Christmas 2021

Dear Friends,

One of the most frequent questions an author is asked is "Where do you get your ideas?" Because my God-given gift is storytelling, I've never been short on those. Story is everywhere I look. Life throbs with it. Inspiration comes from a variety of places: a newspaper article, an overheard conversation, a movie, or, in the case of *Dear Santa,* a chance encounter with an eleven-year-old girl.

My husband's cousin brought her granddaughter, who wanted to be an author, to meet me. When I asked her when she had decided she wanted to write books, she paused, gave her answer thoughtful consideration, and said, "I knew when I started writing Santa letters." Right away, the idea for a book titled *Dear Santa* leaped into my mind.

My Christmas wish is that you enjoy reading about Lindy and Billy. I set the story in Wenatchee, Washington, which is said to be the Apple Capital of the World, something my hometown of Yakima highly disputes, claiming our fair city is the Apple Capital of the World. Each city has an abundance of orchards and a growing number of vineyards that produce award-winning wines.

As always, hearing from my readers is one of the delights of writing books. You can reach me through all the media platforms. Or if you choose to write: my address is P.O. Box 1458, Port Orchard, WA 98366.

Merry Christmas,

Debbie Macomber

Debbie
MACOMBER

Dear
Santa

SPHERE

SPHERE

First published in the United States in 2021 by Ballantine Books,
an imprint of Random House, a division of
Penguin Random House LLC, New York
First published in Great Britain in 2021 by Sphere
This paperback edition published by Sphere in 2022

1 3 5 7 9 10 8 6 4 2

Copyright © Debbie Macomber 2021

A CIP catalogue record for this book is available from the British Library.

ISBN 978-0-7515-8090-7

Papers used by Sphere are from well-managed forests
and other responsible sources.

Printed and bound in Great Britain by Clays Ltd, Elcograf S.p.A.

MIX
Paper from
responsible sources
FSC® C104740

Sphere
An imprint of
Little, Brown Book Group
Carmelite House
50 Victoria Embankment
London EC4Y 0DZ

An Hachette UK Company
www.hachette.co.uk

www.littlebrown.co.uk

To Patt and Steve Boothe,
wonderful neighbors
and even better friends

Dear Santa

CHAPTER ONE

"Home." The moment Lindy Carmichael turned down Apple Orchard Lane in Wenatchee, Washington, she released a deep sigh. An immediate sense of familiar warmth and welcome filled her. She had two full weeks off to celebrate Christmas and New Year's with her family. If ever she needed a break, it was this year. And what a truly terrible, awful year it had been.

Three years ago, after working for several small companies, Lindy had been hired for her dream job with a marketing and website design company. Her degree in computer science, with a specialty in graphics and visualization, plus her work history, was tailor-made for Media Blast. Confident that her creative talent would be a company asset, she'd been sure she'd fit right in. While she loved her job and the opportunity it afforded her, she couldn't help feeling underappreciated. Just before Lindy left for vacation, she'd submitted a campaign for the Ferguson Group, one of their largest accounts. This opportunity to prove her worth was exactly what she'd been waiting for. If her proposal was chosen, then she would get the recognition she deserved. Lindy had never been a quitter. Her dad had once told her that if she did more than she was paid to do, her hard work would eventually be noticed. With time, she'd be rewarded for what she did. Lindy held on to that philosophy and had given this job her all.

Pushing thoughts of work problems from her mind, she pulled in to the driveway of the home where she'd spent the majority of her life. Twinkling lights lining the edge of the roofline greeted her, along with twin reindeer who stood guard over the snow-covered lawn. A large evergreen wreath with silver and blue bulbs hung on the front door. Home for Christmas. This was exactly what she needed to escape the doldrums that had plagued her over the last six months.

Lindy hadn't completely exited her car before the front door flew open and her mother and Beau, the family dog, hurried toward her on the freshly shoveled driveway. Her mother's arms reached for Lindy, while Beau braced his front legs against her thighs, tail wagging, craving her attention. With barely enough time to inhale the shockingly cold air, Lindy was pulled inside the warm house by her mother, who then enveloped her in a full-body hug. Beau barked his welcome, running circles around her, yipping his excitement.

"I didn't think you'd ever get here," Ellen Carmichael said, helping Lindy off with her coat. "How was the pass? I checked the weather conditions, and it was snowing over Snoqualmie. Did you have any trouble? I worry that you don't have snow tires . . . I realize you don't need them living in Seattle, but it's a must this side of the mountains."

"Mom, my goodness, give me a minute to catch my breath," Lindy said, giggling. Home. To be surrounded by love was what she needed most. The kitchen was warm, and her mother had a batch of freshly baked cookies lined up in rows on the countertop. Baking was an expression of love in Lindy's family. Her mother started early for the annual Christmas Eve gathering with longtime friends. Each family would leave with an overflowing plate of homemade cookies.

"Did you eat breakfast?" her mother asked her, as she reached for the coffeepot.

"No. I wanted to get on the road as soon as it was daylight." Traffic over Snoqualmie Pass could be a problem in winter, and it was often closed due to avalanche concerns. Lindy felt the earlier she got out of Seattle and to the other side of the mountain, the better.

"Then sit down and I'll fry you up—"

Lindy cut her mother off, eyeing the cookies on the countertop. "Coffee and a couple of those thumbprints will carry me until lunchtime."

Her mother opened the cupboard for a mug, while Lindy helped herself to her favorite Christmas cookies.

Sitting across from her, Lindy smiled at her mother. This was what she'd held in her mind for the last several months while she weathered the storms life had tossed at her. Home and Christmas. This was the perfect combination to help her out of this deep emotional slump.

Her position with Media Blast was only the tip of the proverbial iceberg. Not wanting her mother to fret, Lindy had kept the majority of her various troubles since summer to herself. Nor was she looking to share them the minute she arrived home. Maybe in a few days, after she'd soaked in the serenity of being at home, she would feel inclined to explain.

After sampling the first cookie, Lindy closed her eyes. "I swear I could eat a dozen of these."

"But you won't. I have lunch planned."

Only then did Lindy notice the simmering pot on the stove. "Did you make pasta e fagioli?" The soup, made with cannellini and kidney beans and small pasta simmering in a rich tomato broth, was a family tradition.

"With sourdough buns," her mother added. The starter

had been handed down from her father's grandfather, who'd once lived in Alaska. He claimed it came from an old Klondike miner and had been kept alive since the 1890s. Lindy knew her parents had shared it with various family and friends. For as long as she could remember, Lindy's father had made sourdough pancakes every Sunday morning for breakfast. On special occasions, her mother baked the buns, using a recipe that had been passed down from her grandmother.

"Mom," Lindy said and groaned, "you're going to spoil me."

"That's exactly what I intend to do. It's been far too long since you've been home."

"I was here for the Fourth of July," she reminded her. She'd come home shortly after getting her own apartment, and just before she'd learned the terrible truth about . . . She stopped her thoughts, refusing to let them drift toward even more unpleasantness.

"Yes, and that was months ago. It isn't like we're a thousand miles apart. Seattle is barely three hours away in traffic."

"I know, I know, but I moved, remember, and then there was this project for work that demanded nearly every weekend. But it was worth it, because I earned two weeks off to spend the holidays with you, Dad, Chad, Ashley, and Peter." Her younger brother had married his high school sweetheart and worked at the apple warehouse in supply-chain management. Within a year, Ashley and Chad had presented her parents with an amazing grandson. Lindy was crazy about four-year-old Peter. They connected every week through FaceTime, and she mailed him gifts so often, Chad had to ask her to resist. Ashley was currently pregnant with a little girl they had decided to name Grace. She was due to arrive the first week of March.

When Lindy finished her coffee and cookies, she unloaded her car and brought her suitcase into her bedroom. Standing in the doorway to the familiar room, she found it exactly as it'd been when she'd left for college. She sat on the edge of her bed and looked around, remembering how carefree life had been when she was a teenager.

A poster of the Jonas Brothers was tacked to one wall. Her pom-poms from dance team were tucked against the corner of the bulletin board, and the corsage she'd worn to her senior prom was pinned to the board.

Home.

Peace washed over her, as she wrapped all that was familiar around her like a heated blanket.

"Lunch will be ready soon," her mother called from the kitchen, soon after Lindy had unpacked. She tucked the few wrapped gifts she'd brought with her under the Christmas tree that adorned the living room, in front of the picture window that looked out over Apple Orchard Lane.

"I'll be right there." After admiring the tree, Lindy joined her mother, who had already dished up two steaming bowls of soup. The breadbasket sat in the middle of the table, along with a butter dish.

After a simple grace, Lindy lifted her spoon. "I dreamed about this soup. It never tastes the same when I make it, and I follow the recipe to the letter. Somehow it always tastes better when you cook it."

"That's because it's made with love."

Lindy wanted to discount this extra ingredient that her mother insisted made the difference. How could she, though, when there didn't seem to be any other explanation?

Her mother waited until Lindy had finished her lunch before she paused, her eyes serious. Looking directly at Lindy, she said, "I'm waiting."

"Waiting for what?" Lindy asked.

"Waiting for you to tell me what's going on with you, and please don't try to brush this off. You'd best tell me before—"

"Mom . . . there's nothing."

With narrowed eyes, her mother waved her index finger like a clock's pendulum. "Lindy Rose, I'm your mother. No one knows you better than me. I've suspected for quite some time you're unhappy. Now spill."

Lindy was afraid that once she started, she might not be able to stop.

"It's more than work, isn't it?"

Her mother did know her. "Yes," Lindy confirmed. "There's more to the story of my split with Brian." Lindy had told her parents they'd broken up, but she hadn't gone into the details. She couldn't. It was too painful then, and only a little less so now.

"You were rather vague about the reasons."

With cause. A majority of what happened were things she'd prefer to keep to herself.

"Did it have to do with you getting that apartment?"

Apparently, her parents were good at reading between the lines. Lindy nodded. It was that and so much more.

"I remember in July that you mentioned your relationship with Brian had changed. It was not long afterward that you decided to go your separate ways."

Shortly after she returned to Seattle Lindy had learned the truth about Brian and Celeste, and it had devastated her.

"You cared for him. Right?"

"Yeah." Lindy had. Deeply. Early in their relationship, she could see them marrying and building a life together, once she'd achieved her career goals. She enjoyed his company, but as time progressed, she could see Brian wasn't ready for marriage, and, for that matter, neither was she. Marriage was a huge commitment.

"Are you sorry the two of you broke up?"

"Definitely not," she said emphatically.

Her mother's eyebrows rose close to her hairline. "Your reaction tells me there's a whole lot more going on that you haven't mentioned."

Lindy's shoulders slumped slightly. She hadn't intended to get into this quite so soon. Now, with her mother probing for answers, Lindy felt like she didn't have a choice. She might as well get it over with. Learning what Celeste, her onetime best friend, and Brian had done wasn't something she relished telling her mother.

Her mother paused as she waited for Lindy to continue. Lindy knew her mother intended to give her time until she was comfortable enough to explain.

"When the lease on Celeste's and my apartment was close to being up," Lindy said, after several pain-filled moments, "we knew it was time for us each to get our own place."

Lindy's heart actually hurt as she relayed the events of the summer.

"Celeste was working in Edmonds. That meant she had nearly an hour commute through the heavy Seattle traffic. It made sense for her to look for an apartment closer to her job. Apartments in Seattle are at a premium, but I found one pretty easily." It was in an older complex, and a friend who was moving had told her about it. Lindy quickly snapped it up. "Celeste wasn't so lucky. It took us weeks to find a place she could afford. She saw one she liked that was out of her price range and went for it. I figured she was better at budgeting than I realized."

Her mother continued to listen, not asking a lot of questions, which Lindy appreciated.

"We made plans to move, vowing to stay in touch no matter what." They'd been roommates and best friends since their college days, and had met during their freshman year. It would be the first time they'd lived apart since they were eighteen.

In retrospect, Lindy should have known something was wrong.

"Celeste signed a lease on an apartment she couldn't afford?"

Lindy nodded, avoiding eye contact.

"How did she manage that?"

"She got a roommate," Lindy said.

"For a one-bedroom unit?"

Lindy glanced up. "She'd met a guy."

"I didn't know Celeste was in a serious relationship."

"I didn't, either." That was the crux of it. Lindy had been oblivious to what was happening between her best friend and Brian.

Her mother frowned. "What aren't you telling me?"

"Her roommate is Brian. The two of them had been

going apartment hunting behind my back for weeks. I was stupidly blind, trusting them both."

"No!" Her mother gasped. "Brian moved in with Celeste?"

Even though she'd learned the truth months ago, a sick feeling churned in Lindy's stomach.

"Well, that weasel."

"That's not the worst of it. Earlier, when Celeste and I decided it was time for us to find our own spaces, Brian had suggested the two of us move in together. I turned him down. I wasn't ready for that kind of commitment. Then, all of a sudden, he called and canceled several dates we'd made. I thought it was his passive-aggressive way of getting back at me for refusing to share the apartment."

"He's a jerk, Lindy. A real jerk."

Her mother's words were tame compared to how Lindy thought of her ex-boyfriend's actions. "Shortly after we moved out of the apartment, I stopped off to see about helping Celeste unpack. I hadn't heard from her since the move and knew she was working long hours and could probably use the help. I'd sent her a couple of text messages that she hadn't responded to, and I was concerned. Imagine my surprise when I arrived and Brian answered the door."

"Oh, Lindy, I'm so sorry."

Lindy had no intention of discounting the betrayal

she'd felt in that moment. It was bad enough that Brian had cheated on her with Celeste, but for her best friend to go behind her back this way was even worse.

Heartache from a broken romance was something she'd experienced before. Johnny Bemis had broken her heart when she was in high school. Her friends had rallied around her, and she'd gotten over him quickly.

This was different. To lose her best friend, her confidant, the one person in Seattle who supported and believed in her, was a double hit. She missed Celeste's company far more than she did Brian's. Even now, it was hard to believe Celeste would betray and deceive her this way. So much for the friends' code of honor.

"It stinks," Lindy said. "The thing is, Mom, I'm a complete romantic failure." Saying it aloud made it seem all the more real.

"Don't say that."

"How can I not? Mardelle and Nate are engaged and have already adopted a dog they named Oscar. She asked me to be a bridesmaid in her wedding this summer. And Mardelle isn't the only one of my college friends who is in a committed relationship."

"I know what Celeste and Brian did hurts."

"No kidding." She hadn't meant to blurt out all this drama the instant she walked in the front door. Lindy had hoped to put all this behind her and enjoy the holidays with her family. The less she thought about Brian and Celeste, the better all around.

"I'm sorry you had to go through this." Her mother's gentle sympathy helped ease the ache in her heart.

"Thank you, Mom. While my head knows that, my heart is having a hard time accepting it."

"I can understand that."

Her mother was right. Still, Lindy found it hard to believe. "It's my own fault. I made the mistake of checking Celeste's page on Facebook last night, and while I was spending my weekends alone, the two of them were skiing on White Pass and attending a Seahawks football game. What hurts most is those are the very activities Brian and I did last winter. I'm such a loser."

"You most certainly aren't a loser, Lindy Rose Carmichael."

"I lost my boyfriend and my best friend. Losing Brian isn't so bad, but Celeste? I have lots of friends, but Celeste and I were so close. We shared everything. I just didn't expect to have to share my boyfriend."

"The two of them deserve each other," her mother said.

Lindy expected her mother to champion her.

"As far as I'm concerned, Brian isn't half the man we thought he was," her mother continued. "It's painful for you now . . . I remember . . ." She paused.

"You remember what?"

Her mother's eyes darkened with sadness. "I remember how I felt when your birth father walked out on me . . . It seemed as if the entire world had collapsed around me. As soon as he learned I was pregnant with you, he took off for the hills. He couldn't get away fast enough."

"Oh, Mom," Lindy whispered. Looking at it from her mother's point of view, Lindy had gotten off lucky.

Scooting back her chair, Ellen gestured for Lindy to remain where she was. "There's something I want to show you."

"Show me?"

"Something that will make you feel better."

While that sounded promising, Lindy wasn't sure anything her mother had to show her would lift her spirits from this funk.

Her mother disappeared and returned a few minutes later. With a big smile, she handed Lindy a child-size shoe box.

"What's that?" she asked, genuinely puzzled, not knowing what to expect.

Her mother's face glowed with excitement. "I went through some of those boxes I packed away in the garage years ago and found this. I've been saving it to show you. These, my precious daughter, are your letters to Santa."

"While they might amuse me, Mom, I doubt they will do anything to take away this ache in my heart."

"I think you might be surprised," her mother insisted. "Now, open it up and read the first letter."

Lindy couldn't imagine anything she'd written back when she'd believed in Santa had the power to influence her life now.

"Trust me," her mother whispered. "Read the one on the top. You wrote it when you were five."

"This is silly." Still, she couldn't help being curious.

"Don't be so sure," her mother said, with a twinkle in her eye.

CHAPTER TWO

Lindy had a hard time believing her childhood letters to Santa had any significance to her current messy life. Nevertheless, she was curious, and reached for the letter at the top of the box.

Opening the envelope, she pulled a single sheet from inside and spread it out on the table. In her childish, awkward print, she'd written:

> Dear Santa,
>   Please bring me a daddy.
>   Lindy

Lindy glanced at her mother and smiled. "I didn't ask for toys? I can remember wanting a bike around that time."

"That came later. All you wanted that Christmas was a dad."

"I don't remember any of this."

"Honey, you were only five. You'd started kindergarten, and for the first time noticed that the other children had fathers and you didn't."

Lindy shook her head. She had little recollection of that Christmas. What she did remember was that bike. As she thought back, she realized her mother was right in that all she had asked for was a dad.

"I remember when I read your letter. No way was I going to be able to give you a father. My heart sank," her mother said. "The only man I'd ever loved had left me. I hadn't heard from him since the day I told him I was pregnant. Through some friends of mine, I learned he'd married someone else shortly after you were born."

"We were far better off without him." Lindy believed that with all her heart. She wouldn't have had the father who loved and raised her if this sperm donor had stuck around, although at the time she understood how his rejection must have badly hurt her mother. Over the years, Lindy hadn't wondered about him herself. Because she was loved by the dad who'd adopted her, she'd never felt the need to know anything about the man responsible for her birth.

"We are much better off," her mother agreed. "Of all

the things you might have asked for, a father was the one thing I couldn't give you. It broke my heart."

"Oh, Mom, I'm so sorry."

"You need to understand. That year, Christmas was bleak. My parents left to spend the holidays with my brother in Kansas, and it was just the two of us. With everything in me, I wanted to make this special for you, because you were going to miss Gamma and Papa."

Lindy knew how dearly her mother loved Christmas, and how hard it must have been for her to be alone, instead of with her family. And then Lindy had to ask for the one thing her mother couldn't provide.

Relaxing against the back of the chair, Ellen's memories returned to that fateful Christmas. With her parents gone, she was alone over the holidays for the first time in her life. She'd done everything she could think of to make it as perfect as she could for her little girl. With a single income, making ends meet was difficult.

Christmas Eve she sat up until nearly midnight, wrapping the few gifts she was able to put under the tree for Lindy. All the while, she regretted that she wouldn't be able to give her beautiful daughter the one thing she'd so desperately wanted—a daddy.

Trust was a huge issue with her, after what happened

with Robbie. He'd said all the right things, lavished her with compliments, seduced her, and then, once he got what he wanted, he changed. His calls became infrequent, and when he did show up there was only one thing that interested him. All the signs were there, only she'd been blind. So blind. His promises were empty, and when she learned she was pregnant, the truth hit her square between the eyes.

How grateful Ellen was for her parents, who loved her and helped support her through the pregnancy. After Lindy was born, they'd helped her get into a small apartment. Robbie had abandoned her and claimed he wanted nothing to do with his daughter. With that attitude, Ellen made the painful decision to cut him completely out of their lives. Robbie was more than happy to sign away all parental rights, which meant he didn't need to pay child support. Consequently, Ellen struggled financially.

Still, she'd been determined to make this a good Christmas for her daughter. Due to her parents' generosity, there were plenty of gifts under the tree for Lindy to open.

Christmas morning, Lindy roared out of bed and raced barefoot to the Christmas tree, sliding toward it like she was running for first base. "Can we open gifts now?" she pleaded.

Ellen brewed herself a cup of tea and smiled as Lindy opened one small gift after another.

"Mommy, look, Gamma and Papa got me a baking oven!"

"Wonderful. You can bake a cake for our Christmas dinner."

Lindy set the gift aside and reached for another package. Tearing away the wrapping, she groaned a sigh. "It's underwear."

"Yes, look how pretty it is."

"No one is supposed to see it, though."

Ellen constrained her amusement. "You're right. You shouldn't show anyone your new pretty underwear."

After three or four presents, Lindy settled back on her feet and looked expectantly at Ellen.

"What's the matter, honey, don't you like your gifts?"

Lindy was quick to nod. "I do. I wanted that bake oven forever and I love the new game and my puzzle. But Santa didn't answer my letter."

"I know, honey, and I'm sorry. Do you want to play with your new game?"

Lindy was quick to agree, and the two played several games before Ellen cooked them breakfast. Afterward, they watched Ellen's favorite Christmas movies and they talked to her parents and brother in Kansas City. Joe asked if his gifts had arrived, and when she said they hadn't, he apologized for mailing them off so late.

When they were off the phone, Lindy mixed up the batter for a small cake to bake in her new oven.

Because it was just the two of them, Ellen roasted a chicken for their dinner. The scent of it drifted through their apartment.

"Chicken is my favorite," Lindy said, as she patiently waited for her cake to finish cooking. She sat in front of the tiny oven and stared at it, watching the small timer tick away.

"Chicken with mashed potatoes and gravy."

"And peas," Lindy insisted.

"And peas." Lindy liked to squish them up with her potatoes and then add the gravy.

It was while she was peeling the potatoes for their dinner that the doorbell rang.

Before Ellen could put down the knife, Lindy was on her feet. "Mommy, Mommy, maybe it's Santa."

Before Ellen could stop her, Lindy raced to the front door and threw it open. "Did Santa send you?" she asked, with wide-eyed expectation.

"I believe he did," the man said, as Ellen stepped out of the kitchen.

"Are you my daddy?" Lindy asked. She whirled around, her eyes bright with joy. "See, Mommy, Santa got my letter after all."

Ellen's face flushed red with embarrassment, and she avoided looking at the man in the doorway.

"Ellen?"

She glanced up and stared. "Phillip? What are you

doing here?" She didn't mean to sound unwelcoming. She'd known Phillip in high school and hadn't seen him since they'd graduated.

"I work for UPS."

She should have realized that, as he was dressed in his brown uniform. "You deliver on Christmas?"

He shrugged. "All the other drivers are married with families. I'm single and volunteered to do the deliveries, thinking some little girl might be waiting for a gift from Santa." With that, he handed the package to Lindy. "I believe this one is addressed to your mom and you."

Lindy grabbed hold of the boxed gift.

Phillip smiled. "I should confess I recognized your name and saved your package for last."

"Please come in where it's warm," she said, when she realized this was his last stop. Ellen remembered that Phillip had always been shy.

"It's just the two of you?" he asked, looking around.

Ellen nodded. "Mom and Dad are with my brother in Kansas City."

Lindy was sitting on the floor, opening the package, which was from Lindy's godmother. Inside was a doll for Lindy and another package wrapped for Ellen.

"I suppose you're in a rush to get back to your family," Ellen said.

Phillip shook his head. "My parents are with my grandparents in Yakima."

In other words, he was alone on Christmas, too. "It isn't much, but would you like to join us for dinner?" Ellen asked. "I mean, if you want. No pressure."

"I'd like that more than I can say." His eyes held hers and they were filled with promise.

Shaking her head to clear the memories, Ellen's gaze returned to Lindy, who was staring down at the letter she'd written all those years ago.

"Dad arrived that Christmas Day," Lindy whispered.

"Yes, it was your daddy, the very daddy you'd asked Santa to bring you."

"I don't remember writing Santa," Lindy said, running her finger over the clumsily drawn letters. "But I certainly recall you and Dad dating and how patient and kind he was to me."

"Don't you remember me saying your dad was the best Christmas present I ever received?"

"Yes, but I had no idea his arrival that day had anything to do with my letter to Santa . . . I mean, that's a stretch, isn't it? More of a coincidence."

"You might not think so, if you read the remainder of the letters."

"I will, but I want to hear more about that Christmas when I was five."

———

Oh, the memories. Phil had returned for dinner after dropping off the UPS truck.

Once again, Lindy hurried to the front door, grabbing his hand and pulling him inside the house. Ellen had the table set and had refreshed her makeup. She remembered the shy looks he'd given her back in school. He'd never asked her out. If he'd found the nerve, she would have gladly accepted.

"Mommy's a good cook," Lindy told him. "Almost as good as Gamma."

Lindy led him to the sofa and then sat down next to him. "I'm five and I can read."

"You must be very smart."

"Do you want me to read you a story?"

"I would."

Ellen was flustered. "Lindy, let's wait until after dinner, okay?"

She looked disappointed but agreed. "Okay. I got pretty underwear for Christmas, but Mommy said I'm not supposed to show it to people."

"Your mommy is a wise woman."

Ellen coughed. If she was wise, she wouldn't have ended up as a single mother.

"She's pretty, too."

"Yes, she is," Phillip agreed. "I've always thought so."

For the next several minutes Lindy chatted away as if she'd saved every experience from the first five years of her life to tell him. He was wonderful, patient, and attentive.

And that Christmas Day was only the beginning. Phillip quickly became a part of Ellen and Lindy's life. And as Ellen had so often said, he was the best Christmas present ever.

"And then later, Dad adopted me," Lindy said.

"That he did. We were married the next summer, and within a few months after our wedding, he legally became your father."

"I'm pretty sure I know why you saved that letter to Santa," Lindy teased.

"Open the next one," her mother urged.

CHAPTER THREE

Reaching inside the small shoe box, Lindy withdrew the next letter. Unfolding it, she spread the paper out on the table and read aloud.

Dear Santa,
   Thank you for my daddy. Mommy has a baby in her tummy, and I would like a baby sister and Rollerblades.

                        Lindy

"I got my Rollerblades, but I didn't get my sister. Instead, we got Chad."

"I don't think you were disappointed, though," her mother reminded her.

"No. The way I figured it, Santa knew what he was doing when he sent Chad. I remember Dad taking me to the hospital to see him. I had to stand on my tippy-toes to look into the nursery. The instant I set eyes on him I knew in my heart of hearts that deep down I really wanted a little brother." Santa had come through after all.

From the time her parents brought Chad home from the hospital, Lindy had doted on him. She couldn't bear to hear him cry and did whatever she could to entertain him. Although there was a six-year difference in their ages, Lindy and Chad had developed a special bond that continued to this day.

"I don't know that I can wait until Thursday to see him," Lindy said. Her brother and his small family came regularly for dinner Thursday night, which was her brother's day off from the warehouse.

"Ashley is only working part-time, so I'm sure if you give her a call, you'll be able to connect."

"Will do." Lindy couldn't wait to see her brother and Ashley, although her nephew, Peter, was the real draw. That kid had had her heart from the first moment she'd held him in her arms. He'd gazed up at her and their eyes had linked. From then on, Lindy was a lost cause.

Chad and Ashley had married young. Chad had told Lindy he knew right away that Ashley would one day be his wife. Even as a teenager, Ashley said she felt the same about Chad. Without question, he was the one for her. If Lindy didn't love them so much, she could almost be jealous.

Intrigued now, she reached into the box for the next letter, opening it and setting it down on the table beside the other two.

Her printing had gotten much better, she noticed. "I wrote this when I was seven," she said, reading it aloud.

Dear Santa,

I'm glad I got a brother instead of a sister. Chad is cute when he isn't crying. I like my Rollerblades, too. I go out every day when it doesn't rain. I want a Magic Marker pen set and a fashion Barbie this year. Oh, and you should give Billy Kincade coal. He's mean. He pulls my hair at school and chases me at recess.

Lindy

Lindy looked up at her mother when she finished reading the letter. "As I recall, I got my wish that year."

"Yes, you did," her mother said. "And you colored until your fingers were every shade of the rainbow."

"What I remember is Chad grabbing my masterpiece and shoving it into his mouth before anyone could stop him."

Memories rolled past her like scenes on a silent movie

screen. She vividly remembered Billy Kincade and how much she disliked him. He'd been a year or two ahead of her in school. Not a day passed when he didn't find some way to torment her. Once he even stole her homework. At recess, he made a point of chasing her. To her, he was the meanest boy in school.

Lindy didn't remember writing Santa about him. At the mention of his name, thoughts of Billy Kincade were fresh in her mind.

"Whatever happened to Billy?" her mother asked.

Lindy didn't have a clue. "I don't remember him beyond second grade. He must have transferred to another school." As far as she was concerned, good riddance. She hadn't thought about him since grade school.

"I remember you complained about him," her mother recalled. "I ended up going to the school principal to find out what the deal was."

"You did?" Maybe that was the reason Billy had transferred schools, not that she cared. Lindy was simply happy to have him out of her life.

"Dad came with me and spoke to Billy privately. Afterward, your father said he felt the reason Billy paid you all that attention was because he had a crush on you."

"If that's true, then he had a curious way of showing it."

"Boys are difficult to understand. It was likely something happening in his home life. Maybe he was attracted to you and didn't know how to show it."

"Save me from boys who have a crush on me, then," Lindy said, thinking of Brian. Nothing had changed through the years, as far as she could tell.

One last letter remained. Lindy was eight at the time.

Dear Santa,

My friend Peggy has a bicycle with tassels and a basket with a flower in the front. Can you bring me one just like hers?

Thank you.

Lindy

Her handwriting had greatly improved by then, she noticed. A smile was hard to hold back as she set aside the letter.

"What's so funny?" her mother asked.

"By eight, I knew Santa was all fun. I wrote that letter so you and Dad knew what I really wanted for Christmas."

"And you got your wish, didn't you?"

"I did, and I loved that bike. Peggy and I rode all over the neighborhood on our twin bikes."

Her mother focused her attention on Lindy. "Have you noticed a pattern here?" she asked, glancing down at the letters.

Lindy's eyes followed her mother's. "Well, other than Santa answering my Christmas wishes, not really." She certainly didn't see anything of significance. While interesting and fun to review, these were nothing more than childish letters.

"Look again," her mother advised.

Lindy glanced down at the four letters in front of her. "What am I supposed to be looking for?" she asked.

"You don't see it, do you?"

Obviously, she didn't.

"When I read your letters," her mother continued, "I noticed nearly everything you asked Santa to bring you, he did. Not always in the way you wanted, but in a way that was better."

Looking over her scribbles, Lindy frowned. "Mom, come on. You and Dad got me all the gifts I wanted."

"To be fair, yes, but remember, you wanted a dad, and Santa sent Phil to our front door on Christmas Day."

"True enough." She couldn't deny it. She'd gotten the daddy she'd asked for, along with a brother. And Billy Kincade had disappeared after she told Santa he deserved coal for Christmas. Plus, she got her own bicycle, the one with pink tassels on the handlebars. She'd ridden it into the ground. While she might not have gotten the sister she requested, she willingly forgave Santa. What she did get was a friend her own age in Peggy.

"You know what I think?" her mother said.

"My guess is that you're going to tell me."

"I think you need to write Santa another letter."

"What? Come on, Mom, don't you think I'm a bit old to believe in Santa Claus?"

Her mother shook her head. "The word you need to seriously consider is *believe*."

Her words gave Lindy pause. She'd been in an emotional rut for so long, it was hard to look at the positive in any situation. Reading those old letters had been fun and they reminded her that at one time she had believed with all her heart. She'd looked forward to each Christmas with happy anticipation, knowing her wishes would be granted.

"After hearing everything that's been going on in your life with Brian and Celeste, plus Media Blast, writing Santa might not be such a bad idea. Maybe a letter letting him know what you'd like most this Christmas is exactly what you need to do. And write it with the same trust you had as a child."

It sounded silly for someone her age to be writing Santa.

"Lindy?" her mother prompted.

"I'll think on it," she said, not wanting to dampen her mother's enthusiasm, and at the same time, finding the suggestion completely ridiculous. She struggled to believe in the magic of Christmas. If anyone learned she'd followed through with such an outrageous idea, she'd be embarrassed.

Later that same afternoon, Lindy helped her mother prepare dinner. Peeling potatoes, she found herself mulling over the silly Santa letters she'd penned as a kid. Her mother was right about one thing. She needed to believe that everything happened for a reason.

She was glad Brian had shown his true colors before their relationship went any further. Although difficult, Celeste should have been honest with her. It would have hurt, but not nearly as much as discovering their betrayal the way she had.

In retrospect, Lindy had to wonder how long they'd hid their affair. Weeks, surely. Weeks before her move, Lindy noticed changes in Brian before Celeste. He didn't call as often, and when they did get together, he seemed distracted. She'd attributed his lack of attentiveness to any number of factors. To be fair to herself, with her work struggles, her mind had been preoccupied.

In contrast, Celeste was her normal cheery self; she hadn't given anything away. It stunned Lindy how naïve she'd been, how trusting. When confronted, Celeste had nothing to say and Lindy didn't seem to, either. After those first awkward minutes, Celeste blurted out that she was sorry. Lindy didn't stick around to hear anything more. She'd left, and they hadn't spoken since, and that had been months ago.

Losing her best friend had been a major blow. They'd been as close as sisters, Lindy thought. Best friends. They'd done everything together for so long that losing Celeste was like missing her right arm. But friends, true friends, didn't betray each other.

If Lindy were to write Santa, which she had no intention of doing, she'd ask for a new best friend. She'd also ask him to send her a new love interest. One with character and substance. A man with integrity. She wasn't so much interested in tall, dark, and handsome. Brian had been all three. Looks didn't matter nearly as much as what was going on inside his heart. A man with heart. In thinking about it, she wasn't sure Santa or anyone else would be able to grant Lindy her wish.

CHAPTER FOUR

The door off the garage opened. "Is my girl home?" Lindy's father asked. He paused long enough to kiss Ellen and then hug Lindy. "Missed you," he said, his eyes full of love.

"You're home early," Ellen said, as she continued to build the dinner salad, adding a sliced pear and chopped walnuts.

Lindy knew that as supervisor of the local UPS center, her father didn't often return home until six or even seven, especially at this time of year.

"I left early. I didn't want to miss out on time with my baby girl."

"Dad, I'm hardly a baby."

"You'll always be my Sweet Pea," he countered.

Yup, this was home, and the love that surrounded her eased the ache in Lindy's heart.

Opening the cookie jar, her dad reached for a thumbprint and headed to the countertop to sort the mail. After he went through everything, he looked to Ellen. "Did you show Lindy the Santa letters?"

"I did."

"What did you think, Sweet Pea?" he asked.

She shrugged. "It was fun going over them with Mom."

"And to think she saved them all these years."

"Astonishing, really," Lindy said.

Lindy spent the evening with her parents, catching up on everything she'd missed since her last visit. Her parents headed to bed at ten, and after calling her brother and planning to connect, Lindy went to her own room. Beau leaped onto her mattress and cuddled up at the foot of her bed. She intended to read as she did most nights. Sitting up in bed, her blankets gathered around her, with a book in her hands was how she normally ended her days. Instead of being drawn into the story, her thoughts drifted over the unexpected events of the day. Most likely, she wasn't going to be able to concentrate.

Turning out the light, she tossed and turned for the next hour, then, giving up, she turned the nightstand lamp on and sat up. Knowing it was useless, she got out of bed, rummaging through her desk drawer until she found a

tablet and a pen. She looked down at the blank page and
wrote:

Dear Santa,

*It's Lindy. I hope you haven't forgotten me after all
these years. Checking in to let you know this hasn't been
the best year of my life. Don't worry, I'm not going to ask
for world peace. My requests should be right up your
alley, if a bit out of the ordinary.*

*Could you kindly introduce me to a man like the one
you brought my mother all those years ago? A man who
values family, and commitment. One who is trustworthy
and honorable, hardworking, caring, and fun. It'd help if
he was fond of children, too. I know he's out there
somewhere, and frankly, I don't want to wait until I get
to heaven to meet him.*

*I could do with another good friend. One I can pal
around with and share secrets. One with a sense of
humor and adventure. Just wondering if you could clone
Peggy?*

*I'm grateful to work with Media Blast and be able to
use the talents God gave me. If I were to have my latest
proposal accepted, I know it would greatly advance my
career.*

*I'll leave it to you to get working on the list and thank
you in advance. You've never disappointed me in the past.*

With her letter written, Lindy felt ready to sleep. A smile came over her as she rested her head against her pillow. Who would have thought she'd think to write Santa beyond the age of eight? Life was full of wonders.

"Did you sleep well?" her mother asked, as Lindy stumbled out of her bedroom at seven-thirty the following morning.

"I did." Truly, she was amazed at how well she had slept. Once she'd written Santa, she'd experienced a feeling of peace. It was probably the silliest thing she'd done in ages, but she couldn't discount the contentment that came over her after she'd penned the letter.

"I've got my book club meeting this afternoon," her mother said, sounding almost apologetic.

Barely listening, Lindy brewed herself a cup of coffee, opening the refrigerator to add creamer.

"It's our Christmas party," her mother continued. "Would you like to join me?"

Leaning her backside against the kitchen counter, Lindy blew into the hot coffee and shook her head. "Thanks, Mom, but if you don't mind, I thought I'd run a couple of errands this morning, and then I'm meeting Chad for lunch on his break."

"Of course. I didn't want you to feel like I was ignoring you."

"Don't be silly. Go and have fun. I'm capable of entertaining myself for a few hours." Lindy was touched by her mother's thoughtfulness, although it didn't surprise her.

After a lazy morning, Lindy met up with her brother at the Wenatchee warehouse. Chad had gotten his degree from Central Washington University in supply-chain management. He'd always had great organizational skills and enjoyed his job.

They headed over to the local diner and talked nonstop for nearly forty-five minutes. Chad filled her in on his and Ashley's plans for the holidays, and Lindy was pleased to know she'd have plenty of time to spend with them and Peter.

Knowing she'd need to update him on her own life, she gave him a brief rundown of what had been going on with her. When he heard about Brian and Celeste, she watched as the anger tightened his face.

"I hate that you had to go through that, sis," Chad said, his dark eyes full of sympathy.

"It's over; I've moved on."

"Good. Glad to hear it."

They hugged outside the diner, and as she walked toward where she'd parked her car, she realized it hadn't been an exaggeration. She felt free of the disappointment and hurt she'd carried on her shoulders these last six months.

Her next stop was at the local dry cleaner. She had a few items she wanted pressed and hadn't had time to have it done before she left Seattle. When she finished, she noticed a Starbucks had opened on the tail end of the strip mall. A peppermint latte sounded good, and she headed in that direction. After ordering a salad for lunch, she was in the mood for something sweet and hot.

As she stood in line, Lindy noticed the tall, slim, fashionably dressed Black woman in front of her. The woman turned to ask her friend something, and Lindy thought she looked vaguely familiar. By the time Lindy placed her order, she was afraid she was staring at the woman, debating if she should introduce herself. No, that was silly. It couldn't possibly be who she thought it was. The only Black person she knew from Wenatchee had been her childhood friend, Peggy. After collecting her drink, Lindy headed for the door, not wanting to look foolish if it wasn't who she thought.

"Lindy, is that you?" The question came at her from the table close to the exit.

"Peggy?" It couldn't be. "Peggy Scranton?"

"Lindy? Lindy Carmichael?"

Lindy started to laugh. Really, what were the chances? "Peggy. Oh my goodness, how long has it been?"

Peggy smiled and gestured for Lindy to join her and her friend. "Since right before middle school."

Peggy had been one of Lindy's closest friends from second grade on. The trouble they'd gotten into was epic. The summer between grade school and middle school, Peggy's family had moved into a new development on the other side of town. Peggy had enrolled in a different school. For the first few months, they were able to keep in contact and maintain their friendship. As time went on, they grew apart. Over the years, Lindy had wondered what had ever happened to her grade school friend.

"This is Jayne," Peggy said, introducing her friend, a blond, blue-eyed woman who looked to be about their age.

"Hi. I'm Lindy."

"Lindy and I were the best of friends eons ago," Peggy explained.

The two started to exchange stories from their youth, entertaining Jayne, who had a bright, easy laugh. "Remember the time we decided to form our own band?" Peggy asked. "We were doomed to failure, since neither of us could play a musical instrument or sing—not that we let that stop us."

"Hey, I can sing," Lindy insisted, "although only rarely on key."

Peggy smiled. "Since we clearly weren't going to make it as rock stars, we launched a neighborhood newspaper."

"A gossip tabloid is more like it," Lindy clarified.

"We certainly didn't lack for originality. Remember that Fourth of July when we decided to put on our own parade?" Peggy asked.

"Indeed, I do." That idea had been one of their few successes. Peggy's two older siblings had come along, and then Chad and his friends had joined the line with their bicycles. Peggy carried the American flag, waving it from side to side as Lindy beat a toy drum. Soon, several of the other neighborhood kids raced to become part of the fun. They didn't have much of an audience, but none of that mattered.

"And remember when you decided to straighten my hair?" Peggy asked. Looking to Jayne, she explained, "Lindy used a flat iron and started my hair on fire."

Lindy nearly snorted her latte, laughing. She'd felt dreadful afterward, and, thinking it would help, she chopped off nearly all of Peggy's hair. Then she had Peggy cut her hair so they would look alike. Even at that early age, she knew she would never make it through beauty school.

After wiping the tears from her eyes, she asked, "You're living here in Wenatchee?"

"Peggy is the editor and journalist for the local magazine *Wenatchee Alive*," Jayne answered. "She does an excellent job, too."

"Oh my goodness, and to think you started your literary career with me as your assistant editor," Lindy joked.

"Jayne makes me sound like I'm writing for *The New York Times*. It's a local publication with a small but dedicated staff.

"What about you?" Peggy asked. "Don't tell me you're here in Wenatchee and it's taken us this long to reconnect."

Lindy shook her head. "Seattle. I'm home for Christmas."

"How long will you be in town?"

"Nearly two weeks, unless I hear back on a proposal I submitted . . . That's unlikely, though."

"Two weeks. Perfect. Just think of the ruckus we can raise in that amount of time."

"You should join us tonight," Jayne said, looking to Peggy, who eagerly nodded agreement.

"What's tonight?"

"Girls' night out," Jayne said.

"We're heading for drinks at the Wine Press."

"Is that a new place in town?" Lindy couldn't remember hearing anything about a new restaurant while she was home last summer.

"It's been around for a couple months now. It's the 'in' place to go for fun."

"And the wine choices are excellent," Jayne added.

"The owner features Washington State wines. It's surprising how many good wines come from our state."

General knowledge told her Washington was the largest wine-producing state outside of California. She wasn't surprised to learn the Wine Press chose to highlight state wineries. It was smart to support the local economy.

"Do you have other plans?" Jayne asked, and seemed genuine in her wanting Lindy to join them.

"Nothing important. I'd love to meet your friends."

"You'll meet Chloe," Peggy told her. "She's a supervisor for Costco."

They stayed and talked for another hour before agreeing to meet later for drinks and appetizers. While they were together, Peggy called and made reservations at the Wine Press for that evening at six o'clock.

Her mother was back by the time Lindy returned from her errands. She must have been smiling when she walked in the door, because her mother commented right away. "It looks like you had an entertaining afternoon."

"You won't believe who I ran into while I was out. Peggy Scranton! We were just talking about her, remember?"

"Peggy Scranton," her mother repeated slowly. "That's wonderful. The two of you were such good friends back in the day."

"Peggy invited me to join her this evening with a couple of her other friends for a girls' night out. Peggy's single and so is Jayne, but Chloe's married." Lindy looked forward to spending time with Peggy's friends. Working the long hours she had on the project for the Ferguson Group, she hadn't been out with friends in ages. Although Lindy hadn't spoken to Peggy in years, it was as if they'd never spent time apart. They both fell right back into the easy friendship they'd once shared.

"I remember when you and Peggy were inseparable," her mother said, interrupting Lindy's musings.

"She was one of my best friends ever."

That evening, as Lindy readied for meeting Peggy and her friends at the Wine Press, she paused long enough to open her nightstand. She removed the tablet with the letter she'd written Santa the night before. One of the things she'd asked Santa was to bring her a new best friend.

"Gotta say, Santa. You're good. You're really good."

CHAPTER FIVE

When Lindy arrived, Peggy, Jayne, and Chloe were already seated. Peggy waved her over, and, following introductions, the server delivered a bottle of wine to their table. With the ease of someone accustomed to opening wine, he removed the cork and filled their glasses.

"The wine is on me," Peggy said, before anyone could argue. "I have my two best friends with me, and I've reconnected with Lindy. This calls for a celebration."

They toasted one another by gently clinking their glasses together. Peggy had chosen a rich red wine with a low tannin that went down way too easy. Lindy looked at the label and decided a bottle or two would make an excellent Christmas gift for her dad, who enjoyed red wine as much as Lindy did.

All the tables around them were full. Peggy had been right. The restaurant was hopping with a brisk business. With the four of them, there was no shortage of conversation. The server returned and asked if they were interested in any of the appetizers.

"Can you give us a few minutes?" Peggy asked.

"Of course, ladies. Take your time."

Once Lindy read the menu, it didn't take her long to decide on hummus with pitas. She'd need food in her stomach before she drank much more wine. Peggy ordered the crab dip and Jayne and Chloe decided to share the spicy grilled shrimp.

A few minutes later, their server returned and took their orders. Lindy added a second bottle of wine to go with their food. She requested another red, this time from a different vineyard.

"Excellent choice," the server said, approving of her selection.

It was as she handed the young man the menu that Lindy happened to notice the name of the proprietor and manager. Will Kincade.

"You know who that is, don't you?" Peggy asked.

Lindy hadn't realized she'd said the name aloud. She shook her head and frowned. "You couldn't possibly mean Billy Kincade, could you?"

"One and the same."

Lindy was shocked. The Billy she knew had been a terror. A bully she'd intensely disliked. Having him move away had been the best thing to happen to her in second grade.

"Billy had a huge crush on Lindy," Peggy explained to Jayne and Chloe.

"If pulling my hair and terrorizing me indicates liking me—I can't imagine what he would have done if he saw me as a threat."

"You might remember I slugged him once, defending you," Peggy reminded her.

Lindy had forgotten that. "You were my hero that day."

"Billy only recently moved back to town," Peggy said, apparently in the know. "From what I heard, he came here from the Yakima area."

"You remember someone from the second grade?" Jayne commented, sounding impressed.

"That's what's so crazy," Lindy went on to explain. Perhaps it was the wine making her head spin. "This is unreal."

"What is?"

Lindy shook her head as if to clear her mind. "When I arrived yesterday, my mother brought out this box she'd found buried in the garage from years ago. Inside were letters I'd written to Santa. I hadn't thought about Billy in forever, but I mentioned him in one of those letters."

"We should ask Billy to come to the table," Peggy said.

Before Lindy could protest, Peggy got the server's attention. The young man quickly returned to their table.

"Is Mr. Kincade available?" she asked.

The server immediately showed his concern. "Was there something wrong with your appetizers, ladies?"

"No, no, not at all. We know him from school. Tell him Lindy Carmichael is here."

"Peggy," Lindy said, and groaned under her breath. "I wish you hadn't done that."

"Go get Will," Peggy insisted.

The server nodded. "I'll check if he's available."

"Oh please," Lindy said, in an effort to stop him, "that isn't necessary. I'm sure he doesn't remember me."

"You wrote Santa about Billy?" Jayne asked. "What did you say?"

This was more than a little embarrassing. "I told Santa Billy didn't deserve any gifts this year and that he should bring him coal instead."

The three laughed.

"It was mean of me, but Billy had intimidated me at school, and I guess it was the only way I could think to retaliate."

No sooner had the words left her mouth than a man approached their table with a welcoming smile. Leaning forward, he braced his hands against the back of Jayne's and Chloe's chairs.

Lindy's mouth sagged open. It was Billy Kincade, the same Billy Kincade from her youth. How she could be this certain, she didn't know. But deep down, there wasn't a single doubt.

Because Lindy was completely tongue-tied, Peggy spoke up. "You remember Lindy, don't you?"

His eyes automatically landed on her with such intensity it made her want to squirm.

"And you were her ardent protector, as I recall," Billy said, grinning at Peggy. "Good to see you both."

"You, too," Peggy said.

Lindy half raised her hand. "Hello, Billy."

She had to admit Billy Kincade had matured into a fine figure of a man. He stood a good six feet tall. If his tight chest and muscular arms were any indication, he was physically fit. His eyes were a deep brown, mirroring the color of her own eyes. His hair was cut close on the sides and long on top, gathered into a neat man bun.

"Did you know Lindy wrote about you in her letter to Santa when she was in second grade?" Chloe said.

Lindy would gladly have disappeared in that moment. The last thing she wanted to discuss was that silly letter. She regretted ever mentioning it.

"Did you, now?" Billy's full attention was focused on her, a smile teasing his sensuous mouth.

"You weren't exactly my favorite person," she mumbled.

Billy crossed his arms and smiled down at Lindy. "And what could I have done to earn your wrath?" he asked, as if he didn't recall a single offense he'd committed against her.

Lindy was convinced he did remember, and she wasn't going to let him pretend otherwise. "You know good and well what you did, Billy Kincade."

"Tell him what you said in your letter to Santa," Jayne urged.

Lindy wasn't interested in confessing her embarrassing childish rant. "It's stupid. Billy doesn't want to hear about that."

"Oh, but I do," he countered.

She should have kept her mouth shut earlier. Given no choice, she confessed. "I asked Santa to bring you a stocking full of coal because that was what you deserved."

"What year was this?" he asked, frowning.

Lindy told him. She was in second grade and he was a much bigger fourth grader.

His face grew tight. "Well, Lindy, you most definitely got your wish. That was the year our father deserted the family. There was no Christmas for Dede or me. Mom had to move us in with her parents in Yakima."

"Oh no." Lindy felt terrible. "I'm so sorry."

Billy's smile lacked humor. "That was a long time ago. Besides, I probably deserved coal instead of presents, so no harm done. Now, if you ladies will excuse me." He left, and Lindy felt the strongest urge to follow him and apologize.

CHAPTER SIX

For as soundly as Lindy had slept Friday night, she tossed and turned on Saturday. The terrible Christmas Billy had had that fateful year kept running though her mind. It was beyond ridiculous to believe her letter had anything to do with what had happened to him and his family. As illogical as it was to assume she was somehow responsible, Lindy couldn't stop thinking about all the ten-year-old had suffered. A child his age couldn't possibly understand what had happened to his father, or why he had left.

When Lindy finally managed to fall asleep, her dreams were filled with Billy Kincade and her as children. She spitefully complained to Santa about him, and in turn Santa promised to make Billy's life miserable. Lindy woke in a sweat when her mother knocked on her bedroom door.

"Are you awake?" her mother asked, opening the door and peeking inside.

"Yes." Lindy sat up in bed and rubbed the sleep from her eyes. She was wide awake now, and grateful for the interruption to her nightmare.

"It's time to get ready for church," her mother told her.

"I thought church was at eleven." That had been the traditional time for worship service for as long as she could remember.

"Pastor added an early service, which we prefer. Your dad said Pastor Dean can't go overtime when he's got another service following on the heels of the first."

"Okay, early service it is," Lindy said, and tossed aside the bedcovers.

"I forgot to tell you about the schedule change yesterday. Then Dad and I were asleep when you arrived home last night. Hope you had a good time with Peggy and her friends."

"The best." After they'd left the Wine Press, Peggy invited Lindy to hang out at her apartment for several hours. It'd been well after midnight before she arrived back home. Renewing their friendship was exactly the boost her Christmas spirit needed. They laughed about old times, and, after reviewing more of their escapades, decided it was probably a good thing Peggy had moved away when she did. Only heaven knew the trouble they would have inspired had they continued on through middle and high school.

After coffee and a quick shower, Lindy was ready to leave for church with her parents.

As she walked out of the house, she noticed a bowl of sourdough pancake batter on the kitchen counter. Her dad had set it up the night before, the same as he'd done when she lived at home. Sourdough rolls and now pancakes. Lindy loved being home.

Church was exactly what she needed to lift her out of the blue funk following her dream. Seeing people she'd known most of her life lifted her spirits, as did singing the traditional Christmas carols. This was the last service before the traditional Christmas Eve candlelight one. Pastor Dean's message was on forgiveness and the necessity of letting go of petty hurts, which was exactly what Lindy needed to hear. Closing her eyes, she released Celeste and Brian, and although it was difficult, she wished them happiness.

After church, as her dad delivered steaming hotcakes to the middle of the table, Lindy eagerly piled four small ones onto her plate and ladled warm maple syrup over the top until the sticky goodness pooled there. Beau took his place beneath the table, hoping someone would be kind enough to share their bacon. Lindy knew her mother had a soft spot for Beau and watched as Ellen slipped him a piece when Lindy's dad wasn't looking.

"How was the food at the Wine Press?" her mother asked. "Dad and I have been meaning to make a reservation, but we haven't had a chance to just yet."

Lindy knew how busy her father was this time of year, so the fact that they hadn't been out often came as no surprise. "The appetizers were great, and the wine selection was diverse in both variety and price." Seeing how busy the restaurant was, there was no doubt it would be a success. "There was only one negative to the night."

"Oh? Wasn't the service good?"

"It was excellent. I happened to meet the owner/manager, and you'll never guess who it is."

"I won't even try. Tell me."

"Billy Kincade."

"Billy Kincade?" her mother repeated, as if she were as shocked as Lindy had been to hear the name. "Not the same Billy you mentioned in your letter to Santa?"

"One and the same. When I recognized his name, I was foolish enough to mention that silly letter. Then, before I could stop her, Peggy asked if Billy would come to our table . . ." She paused before continuing to relay what she'd learned about that horrible Christmas.

"You make it sound like his father deserting the family

was your fault," her dad said, helping himself to another stack of his much-loved hotcakes.

"I do feel that way, and before you say anything, I know that's ridiculous. I could barely sleep last night, and when I did, I had nightmares."

"Billy wasn't upset when you told him about the letter, was he?"

"Heavens, no. What troubled me was when he talked about that Christmas. His eyes grew sad, as if it was one of the worst times of his life."

Her mother grew still and quiet. "You should bake him cookies," she suggested, as if cookies would absolve Lindy of any residual guilt.

"Mom, I don't think Christmas cookies are going to help."

Her dad shook his head. "Don't discount your mother's gingerbread cookies, Sweet Pea."

Lindy was amused and thoughtfully mulled over her mother's idea. Her grandmother's recipe for gingerbread cookies wasn't going to remove the pain she recognized in Billy. She knew that, but at the same time, it was something she could do. A small kindness. She didn't have any plans for the afternoon. Later that evening, Peggy suggested they get together again, possibly take in a movie. Lindy was eager to spend more time with her long-lost friend and had agreed.

———

It was gratifying how quickly Lindy had connected with her friend. It felt like old times. Returning to Peggy's following the movie, they shared wine and confidences. Lindy found it easy to tell Peggy about the situation with her job and her determination to succeed in Seattle. She'd always been driven, but rarely more so than she was with Media Blast. Almost from the first day she'd felt like an outsider. It wasn't until after the first month that she'd learned Laurie, who'd been with the company five years, had also applied for the position. Instead, Media Blast went with Lindy. Feeling their colleague had been cheated, the rest of the team resented Lindy. As a result, Lindy felt the pressing need to prove herself and her qualifications at every turn. After another glass of wine, she spilled the dirt about Celeste and Brian.

Lindy learned Peggy had endured her own heartache. She'd been married then divorced when her alcoholic husband had run up thousands of dollars of debt and then split town, leaving Peggy to deal with the creditors. It had taken her years to pay everything off.

Monday afternoon, just after the Wine Press opened, Lindy arrived with a large plate of gingerbread cookies she'd baked on Sunday. When she'd mentioned what she intended to do, Peggy had agreed with her mother and said it would be a nice gesture. Besides, Billy, with his strong jaw and muscular shoulders, was handsome enough to be on the cover of a romance novel. Peggy seemed to think Billy might still have a thing for Lindy and joked that he might be tempted to chase her the way he'd done when she was in grade school. If that was the case, Lindy was half tempted to let him catch her.

Nice gesture or not, once she arrived at the restaurant, she was nervous. The hostess, a young, attractive woman in her early twenties, greeted her with a welcoming smile. "A table for one?" she asked.

"Actually, I'm here to see Billy Kincade. Is he available?"

"Do you mean Will?"

"I knew him as Billy, but yes, I suppose he goes by Will these days."

"Can I tell him who's asking?"

"Of course. I'm Lindy Carmichael. We're . . . old friends." That was a stretch, but it sounded good. She smiled, hoping it made her look believable.

"If you'll wait here, I'll see if Mr. Kincade is available."

"Thank you." The short exchange didn't ease any of Lindy's nervousness. For half a second, she was tempted to leave. It would be mortifying if Billy refused to see her, once he learned it was her.

She was both relieved and tense when the hostess returned with Billy. He glanced at the plate in her hand and raised his brows in question.

"Lindy?" he said, as if he didn't understand what had prompted her visit. "What can I do for you?"

Thrusting out the plate, she was embarrassed that the hostess was listening in on their conversation. It was bad enough that Billy looked frazzled and impatient. "I baked cookies, because I wanted to apologize," she said, eager to have him take her guilt offering so she could leave.

"Apologize?" he asked, "Whatever for?" He didn't take the plate.

Not wanting anyone to overhear, she leaned forward and whispered, "That letter to Santa."

Billy's face broke into a huge smile. "You're kidding, right?"

"Well, actually, no."

"Come on back to the office. I could use a break. And bring those cookies with you."

He started across the restaurant, leaving her to follow, which she did. His office was compact, and she could see that he'd been sitting at his computer. He brought in another chair and briefly left her.

When he returned, he carried two coffee mugs and they sat across his desk from each other. Glancing appreciatively at the gingerbread cookies, Billy peeled back the cellophane and reached for one. "This wasn't necessary, but it's appreciated. It just so happens gingerbread cookies are my favorite. It's been years since I had homemade ones."

"Grandma's recipe never fails." She ate one herself.

"You can rat me out to Santa every year if it means you'll bake me cookies," he teased.

His humor relaxed her. "You've done a wonderful job with the Wine Press," she said, looking to keep the conversation flowing. "It's clearly a success."

"It might be even more of one, if I could get this website up and running." He glared at his computer, as if to blame the machine for his troubles.

"You're doing it yourself?"

"Yeah. You won't believe what those web designers want to charge me."

Lindy hid a smile. "How's designing it yourself working for you?"

"It's not. I thought if I read a couple books, I should be able to set up a useable web page on WordPress. I mean, how hard could it be? Well, I found out it isn't as easy as it sounds."

"Would you mind if I took a look at what you've done thus far?"

He hesitated. "You want to what?"

"Billy, I design websites for a living. Ever heard of Media Blast?"

He nodded. "They are the top Seattle Web marketing company. I didn't even ask for a quote, because I knew they'd be way out of my price range."

"I work for them. I'd be happy to look at what you have and advise you," she offered, grateful for the opportunity to do more than bake him cookies.

"Before you do, I need to know your fees."

"You're in luck," she said brightly, eager to get started. "The price is more than reasonable. I'll do it for free."

He shook his head. "I can't let you do that."

"Fine, how about a gift certificate for dinner and wine for my parents for Christmas?"

"Done." He quickly vacated his chair and set her up in front of his computer.

It didn't take long for Lindy to assess the work he'd completed and she could see it would require only minor graphic changes but quite a bit of back-end work. He left her and returned later, pacing as he glanced over her shoulder. It didn't take him long to recognize Lindy knew what she was doing. She showed him a few easy tricks and went back to work.

"Do you need anything?" he asked, when he returned later.

Lindy could hear the chatter from the lunch crowd that filled the restaurant. "I'm good, thanks." She didn't move her eyes off the monitor as she worked. It was sometime later that she noticed Billy had delivered a sandwich. Involved as she was, she ate half, hardly aware of what she tasted.

Billy moved in and out of his office several times. He asked how she was doing, and left when she waved him away, promising she was doing fine and didn't need anything. Lindy was in her element.

Her mother phoned to ask if Lindy planned to be home for dinner. Seeing that it was after five, she was shocked to realize how long she'd been working. "Save me a plate. I'm not sure how much longer I'll be," she said, after explaining where she was and what she was doing. Other than potty breaks and a couple of times when she stood to stretch, she was intent on her work.

At seven, Billy insisted she stop. "I'm almost finished," she objected.

"Tomorrow is soon enough."

Although she didn't want to quit, he was right. Her eyes burned from staring at the monitor so long, and her back had started to ache.

"Come with me," Billy said, and scooted the roller chair away from the desk before she could complain.

"Where are we going?" She stood, bent over, and touched her toes to loosen the muscles in her back.

"You ask too many questions." Billy reached for her hand, entwining their fingers. Without answering her, he led her through the kitchen to the far side of the restaurant and into a private dining room. The small round table was draped in a white linen cloth with a ring of holly around a burning candle in the center. A bottle of wine, two glasses, and dinnerware were artfully arranged.

Billy pulled out the chair, silently inviting Lindy to take a seat. Soon after he was seated, two salad plates were delivered by the same server who had taken care of Lindy and her newfound friends on Saturday night.

"What is this?" she asked, leaning close enough to the table for her stomach to press against the edge.

"It's the house salad," Billy said, as if it should be obvious.

"I mean this?" She swung her arm out to indicate the room. "You're feeding me dinner?"

He flashed her a boyish grin. "It's the least I can do, Lindy. You've been working on that design for hours."

"But dinner in a private dining room?"

He glanced around, as if the two of them alone came as a surprise. "So it seems."

Lindy felt like royalty. "Wow. You should know I enjoy my work. This has been fun for me."

"I appreciate your help more than I can say."

"So, tell me, how long have you been in the restaurant business?" Lindy asked. She couldn't help being curious.

"From the time I was sixteen." Billy leaned forward as

he spoke, his gaze warming as he continued. "I started out as a dishwasher for a friend of my grandfather's who owned a diner in Yakima. Eventually I worked my way up, doing every job there was in the kitchen. Earl, my grandfather's friend, taught me nearly all there was to know about the ins and outs of restaurant ownership. I'll be forever grateful to him for mentoring me. I've had other mentors through the years and am grateful for the time they put into teaching me what I would need to know. Earl is the one I owe the most. What about you? How is it you ended up in website design?"

Lindy had always been good with math and science, and that led her to a degree in computer science. The website design and the graphics came about later as she continued her studies. She'd been drawn into the creative part of designing websites, which led her to her job with Media Blast. Without going into a lot of detail, she casually described her work.

"You genuinely love it, don't you?"

"I do," she said. "And if my ideas are chosen on a current project, I will have proved my worth to the rest of the team."

He frowned. "You need to prove your worth?"

"I got hired over someone who'd been with the company several years and expected the position to be hers. She and the rest of the team haven't taken kindly to me."

What she didn't mention was the extra hours she'd put in, the weekends she'd gone into the office, all in an effort to prove that management had made the right choice in hiring her.

"I have to admire your tenacity," Billy said.

"Media Blast is where I've always wanted to work. No way was I going to let a few disgruntled people drive me away."

"Good for you." Lindy didn't mean for the conversation to revolve around her. She wanted to know more about Billy.

"It's fun, running into you, especially after Mom showed me those old letters to Santa."

"You mean to say you'd forgotten me?"

"Not forgotten. Let's just say you slipped my mind."

"I'm here now, Lindy, and happy to see you."

The intensity of his words and the way he looked at her caused her to blush. "Thanks, Billy. It's good to connect with you, too."

Rarely had Lindy enjoyed a dinner more. The conversation flowed easily from one subject to the next. From their work to updating each other about their families.

"You say you're in town for the next two weeks?" Billy asked. "I've enjoyed the time we've spent together. How would you feel about getting together again? It might be at odd hours, though. The restaurant is my first priority.

I'm hoping you won't mind working around that. Would you be willing?"

"That sounds great." Two weeks of letting go and having fun. No way was she turning down this opportunity.

"How would you feel about a trip to Leavenworth?"

"It sounds perfect," she said.

It really did.

CHAPTER SEVEN

The next morning, Lindy couldn't stop thinking about her romantic dinner with Billy. The staff referred to him as Will, but he would always be Billy to her. The evening had been lovely. She enjoyed their conversation and was impressed that he seemed genuinely interested in her and her work at Media Blast. Unlike other men she'd dated—not that they were dating or anything—who had almost always talked about themselves, looking to impress her, she supposed.

It surprised her how much Billy remembered about her and her family. He grinned when he said, "I'm not likely to forget the talking-to our school principal gave me."

"Ah yes, if I remember, that must have been the Billy-the-bully talk," she said, recounting her indignation when he wouldn't let a day pass without pulling her hair.

Like her, Billy had never been married, and while he

didn't mention other relationships, she strongly suspected there had been more than one through the years. It made sense, seeing how attractive and eligible he was.

Coming into the kitchen, Lindy found her mother sitting at the table with the local newspaper and a cup of coffee.

"Sorry about dinner last night," Lindy said, after explaining she'd dined with Billy. Her mother had kept a plate warmed, waiting for her return. By the time she arrived home, the meal had completely dried out. While cleaning up the kitchen, she'd danced around the room, feeling free and a little silly. It'd been a long time since she'd experienced this unfettered happiness. And to think it was all because of Billy Kincade. Covering her mouth, she laughed. Never in a thousand years would she think he'd be the one to make her heart sing.

"No problem, sweetie," her mother assured her. "Were you able to help Billy with his website?"

Lindy nodded as she poured herself a cup of coffee. Her head spun with ideas on how she intended to add the finishing details. "I hope you don't mind if I work on it again this morning," she said. She took the chance that her mother hadn't made plans for them. It was the holiday season, after all, and they had talked endlessly about shopping and baking together.

"I haven't got a thing scheduled," her mother said, convincingly enough for Lindy to believe her.

"I mean if you'd rather—"

"This is your vacation. It's time off you've worked all year to enjoy. You should spend it the way you want. Go help Billy. I'm sure he appreciates what you're doing."

"But Christmas is our time and—"

"Stop," her mother said, smiling at Lindy. "After the year you've had, all I want is for you to enjoy yourself, and if that means working on a website for Billy, then have at it, as long as it makes you happy."

Now was probably the best time to mention his invite. "Tomorrow is his day off and Billy suggested we spend the afternoon in Leavenworth. I hope you don't mind if I go." It would be another day that her mother might have made plans that she didn't know about.

"Lindy, please, go and have fun. Rest assured you're not letting me down."

"You're sure you don't mind?"

"Lindy, when have I ever not spoken my mind?"

She grinned. Her mother had never been one to hold back her opinion.

"I'm happy you've reconnected with Peggy and Billy, too. Now, don't you worry about a thing here. All I ask is that you do what your heart wants."

When she'd left Seattle, Lindy had been in low spirits. What she hadn't expected was to reconnect with Peggy and run into Billy Kincade. From the moment she'd arrived in Wenatchee and read those old letters to Santa, it felt as if the gray world had suddenly turned bright red and green—the colors of Christmas.

"Thanks, Mom."

Her mother glanced up from the newspaper. "You're welcome, sweetie."

When she arrived at the Wine Press, the same young hostess who had greeted her the day before unlocked the restaurant door, as it had yet to open. A flurry of activity was going on inside as the servers set the tables. The kitchen, or what she could see of it, was bustling as well. The aromas drifting toward her convinced her that the latte she'd picked up on her way in wasn't going to satisfy her for long.

"You're back," the hostess said. "Will wasn't sure exactly when you'd arrive. He's with . . . someone currently. I'm sure he wouldn't mind if you went straight to his office."

He's with . . . someone? Lindy frowned at the way the young woman hesitated, as if she wasn't sure she should mention whoever it was who currently occupied her employer's time. That was interesting.

As Lindy wove around the tables, making her way toward his office, she caught sight of Billy leaning against the bar. He was in what looked like a deep conversation with a woman who looked vaguely familiar. A beautiful woman.

Not her business, Lindy decided, and with a determined effort looked away.

Once inside Billy's office, she sat down at his computer and logged on with the information he'd given her. She'd just started working when her phone buzzed.

Even after only a few calls, Lindy recognized the number. Peggy.

"Hey," Peggy said, when Lindy answered. "Do you have plans tonight?"

"What's up?"

"A group of us are going on a food scavenger hunt. Want to join us?"

"A what?" Lindy had never heard of such a thing.

"I'll explain it later. Meet me at my apartment at six."

"Do I need to bring anything?"

"Other than yourself, a bottle of wine, and a white-elephant gift, not a darn thing."

Lindy grinned. She had no idea what a food scavenger hunt was, but it sounded like fun, and she was up for that. "I'll be there."

"See you then."

Lindy disconnected just as Billy entered his office. "Sorry to keep you waiting. I was talking with my sister. You remember Dede, don't you?"

Lindy vaguely remembered her. They'd been in the same school. Dede was a couple of years older than Billy.

"She was a bit older. I remember you had sister, but I don't think we ever spoke," she said, smiling up at him.

"I'm grateful to my sister. I faced some challenges when I decided to open the Wine Press. I couldn't have done it without Dede and her husband, especially after . . ." He let the rest drop.

Lindy was about to ask him what he meant. Before she could, Billy asked, "Were you able to clear tomorrow afternoon with your mom?" he asked.

"We're good."

"Great."

That smile of his was enough to light up a million-kilowatt dam. It took an exaggerated moment before she found the wherewithal to look away. It surprised her how quickly she found him occupying her mind. She'd fallen asleep with thoughts of him, and he was the first thing she thought about when she woke, eager to spend time with him.

When Lindy arrived at Peggy's, Chloe and Jayne were already there, and the party was about to begin. Peggy was the one with the idea: It seemed as if both of the other women were as much in the dark as Lindy was.

Lindy added her wrapped white elephant gift to the stack with the others and handed Peggy the bottle of white wine, one her father had recommended.

Peggy had a sly grin, and Lindy had to wonder what her clever friend was up to now. Even when they were children, Peggy was the one who'd had the wild imagination. Lindy had followed gleefully along. Her childhood had been happy, and a lot of that delight had been the times she'd spent with Peggy. This latest adventure told her Peggy hadn't changed. She was fun, creative, and up for anything.

"Okay, is everyone ready?" Peggy asked. She rubbed her palms together, as if she could hardly wait for this fun evening she had planned.

"As ready as I'll ever be," Lindy said, sharing a look with the other two women.

Peggy passed out a folded sheet of paper to each one. "Okay, read your clue. You have thirty minutes to solve the riddle, and then find and supply the course of the meal described to you. Remember, you have only a half-hour to complete your task. The first one back gets a prize, and the last one back . . . well, let me put it like this: You don't want to be last."

Lindy waited until Peggy's two other friends each had their sheet before she unfolded hers and read the riddle.

Roses are red. Violets are blue.

Dessert, my friend, is on you. Make it sweet and easy to eat.

Not Gouda. Not cheddar. This tastes so much better.

It's a cake most don't bake. Thirty minutes is all it should take.

It wasn't hard for Lindy to figure out that Peggy was looking for her to deliver a cheesecake. She could only imagine what the others had been asked to contribute to the meal. What a fun and different idea. Leave it to Peggy.

"The main course is in the Crock-Pot, and I'll have the wine open and the table set by the time you return. The first one back gets the honor of being the last to choose the white-elephant gift and unable to have anyone take it away."

"And the last?" Jayne asked.

"The last gets to clean the kitchen."

All three groaned as they surveyed the area. It seemed Peggy had deliberately used every pan in the house.

Lindy was excited for what was sure to be a fun evening.

Out the door the three of them flew.

Lindy went to her favorite bakery and found that it was far too busy. Seeing the line inside, she automatically drove past. Naturally, the bakery was her first choice. She'd consider herself lucky if they even had a cheesecake left this late in the day. Keeping a close eye on the time, she saw that she'd wasted five minutes.

Her next stop was Costco. They always had cheesecake, but the parking lot was full. Going inside would be a wasted effort and sure to eat up her time. She should have known. This was the holiday season. Shoppers took every opportunity available to stock up, and this was Christmas week.

Her next guess was the local grocery store. She parked, rushed into the bakery section, and discovered there wasn't a cheesecake to be found.

Then she remembered the Wine Press had cheesecake on the dessert menu. As she exited the Safeway, she reached for her phone and called the restaurant. The same hostess from the morning answered.

"This is Lindy . . . Would it be possible to speak to Billy?" she asked, checking the time and fearing she was about to get the booby prize.

It seemed to take forever before he was on the line. "Lindy?"

"I need four slices of cheesecake. Pronto."

His hesitation was brief. "Is there a cheesecake emergency I didn't hear about?"

"It's a food scavenger hunt. Peggy's idea. If I don't have

it within the next few minutes, I could be stuck washing a sink full of dishes. Can I buy the cheesecake from you?" At this point she didn't care what it cost. All that was important was that she return with the dessert before Jayne and Chloe.

"Of course."

She looked at the time again. "I have less than twelve minutes to get it back to Peggy's."

"Where are you now?" he asked.

She gave him her location.

"I'll meet you halfway." He gave her the name of the school, the very one they had attended as children. "I'll meet you in the parking lot by the baseball field."

"You mean it's still there?"

"As far as I know. Seems to me I drove past it recently."

"You'd leave the restaurant and rush me the cheesecake?" She was giddy, knowing this was the only way she'd make it back to Peggy's within the allotted thirty minutes.

"On it. I'll be there as soon as I can manage . . ."

Lindy drove to Mission View Elementary, pulled over, and parked. Sure enough, Billy didn't keep her waiting long. He pulled up alongside her car. Billy climbed out of his vehicle, and without realizing how close he was, Lindy opened her car door and slammed it into Billy, hitting him in the stomach.

Billy gasped and bent over.

"Oh no. Billy, I'm so sorry. Are you hurt?" She felt dreadful. Her hands flew to her mouth as she waited for him to straighten.

He took in a shallow breath. "I'm okay," he said, between gritted teeth.

"You're not," she countered, fearing she'd unmanned him.

He waved away her concern before he handed her the box with the cheesecake. "How much do I owe you?"

"It's on the house."

"But . . ."

"You did me a favor and I'm returning one." He still didn't sound like himself.

"You're hurt," she insisted. "What can I do to help?"

"Lindy, I'm fine. You caught me by surprise is all."

"You're hurt."

"I am not hurt. You better get going or you'll be washing dishes."

"Right. You're sure you're not in pain?"

He arched his brows, which she supposed was answer enough.

"Now go."

"Right." Still, she hesitated, fearing he was just telling her he was unhurt when he really was in pain. She waited until he was in his car before she left.

Lindy arrived back at Peggy's apartment, with three minutes to spare. It was funny because Jayne arrived almost the same time but was a few steps ahead of her. She discovered Jayne was responsible for the appetizer: Chinese eggrolls. Chloe came within a minute or two of Lindy. Chloe had been given the riddle for the salad: Waldorf, which made sense, since it included apples, the primary crop of Chelan County. How the two had managed it within the limited amount of time was beyond Lindy, knowing her own difficulty in getting the cheesecake.

Peggy greeted them in the kitchen. The table was set with Santa plates and napkins. With the food on the table, the fun began as they relayed their adventures over crisp white wine and laughter. Peggy's own contribution to the meal was taco soup, so it was truly an international meal.

"Waldorf salad?" Chloe complained. "Really, Peggy? Couldn't you have gone for one a bit less specific?"

"Where in the name of heaven did you find that?" Lindy asked.

Peggy laughed. "Her mother is famous for the salad. I figured, it being this close to Christmas, she would have made it for the family."

"Yes, and I stole it, which means I might well be disowned. If I lose out on my inheritance because of you, Peggy, I'll never forgive you."

Lindy told of her own madcap time to find the dessert. She described how Billy had helped and how she had shoved the car door into his midsection. "I'm afraid I might really have hurt him. Being a guy, he would never admit it, though."

"We should check on him later," Peggy suggested.

Lindy agreed.

Dinner was fun. They sat around Peggy's table and talked and laughed for hours. Lindy felt as if she'd known Peggy's two friends forever. They made her part of their fun group, willingly including her as a friend.

Chloe had to get home to her husband and children, and Jayne had to work early in the morning. Lindy was the last to get ready to leave.

"You still want to check up on Billy to see if he's okay?" Peggy asked.

"I think I should."

"I'll go with you."

They drove in separate cars. The parking lot wasn't nearly as full at the Wine Press, now that it was long past the dinner hour, although the lounge seemed to be doing a healthy business.

Billy was behind the bar, talking up the wine with an engrossed audience. When he saw Lindy and Peggy, his face broke into an automatic grin. He motioned for them to join him at the bar.

They were fortunate enough to find two empty stools next to each other and claimed them. Breaking away from the small group he'd been chatting with, Billy approached Peggy and Lindy. He automatically placed napkins on the bar in front of them. "What can I get you ladies?"

"I came to see if you were injured," Lindy said. She'd worried about him all night.

"I'm fine," he said, garnering the attention of those sitting at the bar.

"You had a car door slammed into you."

"I'm fine," he said again.

Lindy remained unconvinced. "Are you positive?"

Shaking his head, Billy sighed loudly to the couples on either side of Peggy and Lindy. "All together now," he said, raising his land like a maestro with a baton ready to lead an orchestra.

In unison, those at the bar said in one voice:

"He's fine!"

CHAPTER EIGHT

Billy came to the house to pick Lindy up for the short twenty-three-mile drive to Leavenworth. As a child, her parents had taken the family to this German village for their annual Oktoberfest, which was one of the largest in the country. The town's Christmas celebration was even bigger.

People came from all over the world to this tiny burg during the holiday season. The city's festivities had become popular long before being highlighted on national television. What had always amazed Lindy was the story behind the city. Many years ago, Leavenworth had been in trouble. Recognizing they needed to do something to boost revenues before the small town, nestled in the foothills of the Cascade mountains, became a ghost town, the city council decided to reinvent Leavenworth. They succeeded beyond what anyone could imagine.

Lindy's mother greeted Billy at the front door while Lindy gathered her coat and purse. "My goodness, Billy," Ellen said, shaking her head as she looked at him. "You've grown so tall."

"Mom, the last time you saw Billy he was ten. It's only natural he'd grow."

"But to over six feet?"

"Height runs in the family," Billy said, sharing an amused look with Lindy.

"I think it's time we go," Lindy suggested, before her mother said something that would embarrass her or mentioned that infamous letter to Santa.

Her mother appeared highly entertained by the two of them. "Off with you, then. Have fun, you two, and don't worry about the time."

"Yes, Mom." From the way her mother acted, one would think Lindy was still in high school and needed to be home before her curfew.

To her surprise, Billy reached for her hand as they walked toward his car. Not that she objected. The warm feelings that ran through her at the simple gesture could be described only as welcoming.

Once inside his four-door truck, Lindy noticed that Billy had turned on the heated seats. Snow had been predicted at the higher elevations, which meant it was likely to snow in Leavenworth, as well as in Wenatchee.

Billy headed through town to U.S. Highway 2 for the thirty-minute drive to the German town. "I was able to get us dinner reservations at Berghoff's," he mentioned, as if all that was required was a phone call.

"No way." The German restaurant was often booked months in advance, especially at this time of year. The food was legendary.

"The owner is a friend of mine," Billy explained. "He moved a few things around to fit us in. The reservations are for six, which should work perfectly for the day I have planned."

Billy had made other arrangements, or so it appeared. "And pray tell, what do you have scheduled?"

He briefly took his eyes off the road to glance her way. "The usual. A sleigh ride, a visit to Santa."

"A visit to Santa? You're kidding, right?"

"Nope. It seemed appropriate, seeing how you appear to be on his list, and how often you wrote him as a kid. I figured you'd welcome sitting on his lap again and telling him what you'd like for Christmas."

"Very funny," she chided, with more than a hint of sarcasm. "I'm too old to be chumming up with Santa," she said, and then she remembered her most recent letter to the jolly old fellow, where she'd asked for a new best friend. The ink was barely dry on the page when she'd re-connected with Peggy. And that wasn't all. She'd run into Billy, too, when she'd asked Santa to introduce her to a worthy man.

"Too old for Santa?" Billy teased. "Is anyone really too old for Santa?"

"You're right," she agreed. "Maybe visiting Santa isn't such a bad idea after all." Impulsively, she leaned her head against his shoulder. She knew this day was in apprecia-tion of the work she'd done on the website for the Wine Press and nothing more. A relationship with Billy wouldn't really work beyond these two weeks, which was unfortu-nate. She had her life in Seattle, and he was a restaurant owner in Wenatchee. Weekends, when she was off work, were his busiest days of the week. He couldn't drive to Seattle to be with her. Furthermore, his attention had to be on his business, if she were to come to spend time with him.

Far better for her to tone down the attraction she felt for him. Even Billy seemed to understand this time could be for only these two weeks; anything beyond Christmas would be problematic. Nevertheless, a short holiday ro-mance would certainly lift her spirits. Being with Billy helped relight the smoldering flame of hope in her heart. That was all this attraction could ever be. Keeping it light and fun would work best for both of them.

When Billy pulled into the alleyway behind the German restaurant, she had to acknowledge he had great connections in town. He parked behind Berghoff's in a space his friend had saved for him. The small town had precious little parking available, and people who drove often had to walk several blocks to the center of town, where many of the activities took place.

Just as he turned off the engine, the snow started to fall in light flakes, drifting down from a flat gray sky. Climbing out of the truck, Lindy looked up and caught several fluffy flakes on her nose.

"Remember as kids how we used to catch the snowflakes on our tongues?" Billy asked.

"I do." Snow in Seattle, a city on the water, didn't often get the experience. Snow, three days before Christmas, was a treat to be treasured.

When they made it onto the main thoroughfare, it came as no surprise to be caught up in the thick crowds of tourists. Several of the stores on the main street had hired someone to stand outside to count the number inside the business. It was essential because of the fire codes. The requirement to wait before shopping certainly didn't seem to dampen the holiday spirit. Street vendors loudly peddled roasted chestnuts, fancy coffee drinks, steaming cups of hot chocolate, and homemade doughnuts.

The train from Seattle whistled as it drew near town.

Many tourists from the west side of the mountains opted to take the train rather than risk driving over the mountain pass that led to Leavenworth. These family adventures were highly popular for those coming from the metropolitan area. The train arrived at various times and then returned to Seattle, making it a perfect day trip.

The giant clock in the center of town chimed musically as the snow lazily drifted down upon them, leaving a layer of white on the shoulders of her bright red wool coat.

"To the sleigh ride first," Billy said, gripping her gloved hand. As before, she felt an instant warmth at his touch. She ignored the warning from earlier, to guard her heart, determined to enjoy every minute with Billy.

The line for the ride was long, snaking down the pathway. Lindy counted some twenty couples ahead of them. She didn't mind. Everyone appeared to be in a jovial mood, filled with the holiday spirit. A group of Victorian-dressed carolers walked past, their voices blending in perfect harmony. Her attention drifted to the train that sluggishly edged toward the depot and pulled to a stop.

Lindy's gaze followed the passengers as they disembarked. As she suspected, they included several families. Parents with young children, eager to explore the city. The eager youngsters leaped onto the platform, their voices raised in excitement. The Victorian carolers were there to greet them with a song. One little girl who couldn't be more than about five or six stared up at the quartet, her eyes wide with wonder.

Standing behind her, Billy placed his hands on Lindy's shoulders as the line progressed toward the horse-drawn sleigh. The romance of this outing didn't escape her.

"It won't be long now," Billy said, whispering close to her ear. They were only two couples back from the front.

As she turned to smile at him, her gaze went naturally toward the train platform and the little girl. Then something past the child caught her attention. Lindy's eyes widened when she saw Brian and Celeste step off the train.

No way.

What were the chances that the two of them would arrive in Leavenworth at the same time she was there? She watched as Brian helped Celeste off the first step. He'd always been the gentleman . . . until he wasn't. A shiver went through her. She'd assumed that because she'd forgiven them, this sense of loss and betrayal wouldn't feel like a kick in the stomach. She inhaled a deep breath and refused to let her thoughts wander down those rut-filled paths.

"Are you cold?" Billy asked.

He must have felt her stiffen. "A little," she said, rather than go into any details. She purposefully looked away, determined not to let Celeste and Brian ruin her day. If they saw her with Billy, then all the better. That would assure them she had moved on, and she had.

Billy rubbed his hands down the sleeves of her coat in an effort to warm her. "We'll be under those wool blankets in a matter of minutes," he said.

"It won't be long," she agreed, as they drew steadily closer to the front of the line.

When their turn came, the young man who was the assistant motioned for Lindy to climb onto the sleigh. Billy had climbed aboard first and offered his hand, which she gladly accepted. As soon as she was seated, he pulled the heavy blankets over her lap and wrapped his arm around her.

Warmth infused her. First from the blankets, and second, from her proximity to Billy. Not only was he attentive, but he was thoughtful, too. The horse and driver took off down a well-worn, snow-packed path into and through the thick woods. The horse's hoofs kicked up a light dusting of the freshly fallen snow. Christmas music swirled around them and then gradually faded as they continued into the forestland. Their driver chatted amicably as he flicked the reins against the horses.

"Your first time in town, folks?" he asked.

Billy looked to Lindy to answer. "No. First sleigh ride, though."

"Good to have your sweetheart with you."

"Very good," Billy answered, smiling at Lindy.

Mesmerized by the glow in his eyes, she smiled back and snuggled closer.

The wait, as Lindy suspected, was longer than the ride. Not that it mattered. The few minutes they were in the forest were magical. This was everything Christmas was meant to be. With Billy at her side, and his arm protectively around her. The fir trees that lined the path, their limbs burdened with the weight of the snow, created an iconic winter wonderland. Music from the carolers faded and then returned as they neared the starting point.

As they made the final turn, Lindy noticed Brian and Celeste were in the line, but not close enough that they would easily see her and Billy. She would really rather not run into them.

"You're chilly again," Billy said.

As the sleigh drew closer to the drop-off point, she turned to look at Billy. "Would you do something for me?"

"Sure. What do you need?"

"Would you kiss me?"

His smile was huge, and he didn't hesitate for even a moment. Capturing her face, his hands covering her ears, he slowly lowered his mouth to hers.

Lindy wasn't sure what she'd expected when she'd made the request. One thing was certain, it wasn't the intense emotions that quickly laid claim to her. At first Billy's lips were cold, which only made sense, seeing as they'd been riding through below-freezing temperatures. His mouth warmed quickly as he deepened the kiss. Heat spread through her as she opened to him, raising her arms to rest her hands on his shoulders. She quickly became involved in the kiss. Slanting her head to one side, she was lost in the wonder of the moment. The magic of it. The sensation of being in his arms, as if this was where she had always belonged.

When they broke apart, all they seemed capable of doing was staring at each other, as if they were both shocked by the intensity of the kiss. Lindy could hear the people clapping and a few shouts and cheers directed toward them long before the sleigh came to a stop. For a moment, she didn't hear the young man urging them to climb off the sleigh.

As he had earlier, Billy went first and then helped her down. As soon as her feet were on the ground, she couldn't resist looking toward the line. She could only hope Celeste and Brian had witnessed a kiss that was far and away better than any she'd ever experienced. A smile tickled her mouth as she looped her arm around Billy's elbow.

"Lindy."

Celeste called her name, and when Lindy turned, she could see that she regretted it. Her once best friend lowered her head as if she was embarrassed.

"Celeste," she said, and then nodded to Brian. "The sleigh ride is probably the most romantic thing I've done in ages. You'll enjoy it. Have a fun day." When neither seemed inclined to continue the conversation, Lindy and Billy left.

They hadn't gone far when Billy paused and turned to face Lindy.

"You want to tell me what that was about?"

She toyed with playing dumb and recognized that wouldn't work. Not with Billy. "That was my onetime best friend and my old boyfriend in line."

"So that's what prompted you to ask me for the kiss?"

Shame filled her when she realized how wrong it was of her to use Billy.

"How recent was the breakup with this guy?" he asked, his voice stiff and deep.

"Six months. He moved in with my former roommate, who I considered my best friend," she admitted, and then added, "I apologize . . . I shouldn't have used you. It was wrong of me, but I wanted them both to see that I'd moved on."

"I understand, Lindy, better than you realize. I've had my own share of disappointments from people I've trusted. It's a painful lesson. I'm sorry you had to go through that."

She hoped he did understand. "Asking you to kiss me

seemed like a good idea at the time, but in retrospect, I . . ." She paused, unsure if she should continue.

"In retrospect, what?" he prodded.

"All right," she said, shrugging a sigh that raised her shoulders two full inches. "Here's the truth. That kiss was . . ." She struggled to find the words. "Was the best ever."

"The best? Ever?"

"Better than the best. It was wonderful. I might have asked you to kiss me for all the wrong reasons, but Billy, wow. That kiss did something to my heart." She pressed her hand over her chest to reassure him she wasn't just saying that, but she meant it.

"You mean like heartburn?"

"No," she answered, laughing, certain he was making a joke. "As I said at dinner, my job has been a challenge lately, and then the breakup."

"That's understandable."

"Mostly it was my pride that took a beating," she confessed.

"You liked the kiss?" Billy asked.

"Out of all I said, this is what you want to ask me?"

He shrugged. "It didn't do my ego any harm."

Lindy smiled. He was right. The past meant nothing now. He'd asked, and she was glad she'd been honest.

"What are you feeling about that kiss?" She couldn't resist wanting to know.

He gave a lighthearted shrug. "It wasn't bad."

"What?" She demanded, and elbowed him in the ribs.

Billy did a good job of pretending she'd injured him. "Okay, if you must know, the kiss was pretty darn spectacular, although I can do better, given the opportunity."

Lindy wound her arm around his waist once again. "Then I'll make sure you get that opportunity."

"Sounds good to me." He brushed his lips over her forehead.

CHAPTER NINE

"Where to next?" Lindy asked.

"How about some cocoa and a hot doughnut?" They both could do with a bit of warmth in their stomachs.

"I could do with coffee."

While Lindy glanced through the window into the hat store, Billy went for coffee. There were easily twenty to thirty people waiting for a chance to get inside the tiny shop to try on their unique caps, hoods, and bonnets.

He joined her and they were fortunate enough to find a space to sit on the lip that circled the town fountain. At her first sip, Lindy blinked back tears. "My goodness, this is strong. It's a defibrillator in a cup."

"I thought that's what my kiss was."

She smiled as she lowered her gaze to the steaming disposable cup. "Yes, that, too."

"Knew it."

Men and their egos! It felt wonderful to laugh and smile again. If she did happen to run into Brian and Celeste a second time, she wouldn't care. This afternoon with Billy was exactly what her heart needed.

After they finished their coffee, Billy took her hand and led her to the Santa house.

"You know this really isn't necessary, don't you?" she said, feeling more than a little silly.

"I think it is."

Seeing that Billy insisted, Lindy decided to play along. It didn't hurt that she'd recently written Santa a letter, as childish as that might seem. Listing the very things her heart desired had been freeing, especially after reading those early letters she'd penned as a girl.

As they stood in line, Lindy watched Santa with the children. He had the patience of a saint, taking time with each one and listening intently as they reviewed their Christmas wishes. When it was her turn, Santa didn't bat an eye. He held out his hand, welcoming her to join him, and then patted his knee.

"Hello, Santa," she said, smiling at the older man. His white beard was authentic, and he had a twinkle in his eye. Lindy felt ridiculous, as she was the only adult waiting for her turn with the big guy. One of the children in line pointed at her.

"She's too old for Santa," he announced, with righteous indignation.

Santa wagged his finger at the child. "No one is ever too old for Santa," he told the little boy.

He turned and focused his attention on Lindy. With an encouraging smile, he said, "Ah yes, I've been waiting for you."

"Really?" she said, teasing him.

His dark eyes grew serious, as though her doubt had offended him. "I have, Lindy."

He knew her name, but she suspected Santa must have heard Billy say it. From having observed him earlier, she could see he was sharper than other men who stepped into the role.

"Have you been a good girl this year?" Santa asked.

"Absolutely," she said, having a difficult time not giggling. "The very best."

"I'm happy to hear that. Now, what would you like Santa to bring you?"

"Didn't you get my letter?" she teased.

"I'm sure one of my elves has placed it on my desk. I promise I'll read it once I return to the North Pole." He sounded sincere, and she found that rather endearing.

"Good, because it's a heartfelt list."

"I'm sure it is, and I promise to read it soon. But since

you're with me now, why don't you tell me what's on your list this year."

As she visited with Santa, Billy was busy taking photo after photo, moving from one part of the room to another, taking a dozen or more pictures of her on Santa's knee. He seemed to find this amusing, and she let him have his fun. Billy had done everything to make this day special, and she wanted him to know how much she appreciated his efforts.

Seeing her time with Santa was about to end, Lindy said, "Before I go, I want you to know that when I was six, I asked for a little sister, but you sent me a brother instead. I forgive you, because Chad is the best little brother a big sister could ever want. So, thank you."

"You're welcome. I'm sure it was a mailroom error. The elves must have confused your letter with another youngster's. That occasionally happens."

Lindy hid a smile at how serious his apology was. "No worries, it turned out for the better."

Santa grinned sheepishly.

"Also, I regret asking you to bring Billy Kincade coal. That was unkind of me."

"Billy Kincade," Santa slowly repeated the name as if testing his memory. "I do remember that young man. He was quite the rascal. I don't suppose you know whatever became of him?"

She gestured across the room. "That's him with the phone."

"My, my, he's grown into quite the fine young man. I'm happy to see you've resolved your differences."

"We have," she said, finding their conversation fun.

Santa handed her a candy cane, and she knew it was time to go.

"Thank you, Santa," she said, and stood.

"You know," Santa said, stopping her. His twinkling eyes held hers for an extralong moment. "That letter you recently wrote me."

"Yes?"

"I'll do my best to make sure all your wishes come true." The smile had left, and once more he held her gaze for an extralong moment.

"Thank you," she said, having trouble finding her voice.

Billy met her at the back of the line and asked, "What did Santa say as you were leaving?"

Now that Lindy thought about it, she found Santa's parting words more than a little perplexing, as if he was serious . . . as if he was sincere. "He said what he does to everyone, I suppose, that he'd work on my Christmas wishes."

Billy reached for her hand. "He looked . . . I don't know, like he was about to ask you out on a date."

Lindy laughed and leaned her head against his shoulder. "That's hilarious."

"Did you tell him your Christmas wish?"

"Not exactly. I told him I wrote him a letter."

"I bet you didn't ask for Rollerblades," he teased.

"No, it was a bit . . . it was personal."

"Got it. And Santa said he'd be working on it?"

"He did." Lindy sincerely hoped he was right. She wanted to make it on her own in Seattle. She had a lot to prove to the team at Media Blast. As for the other items on her list, she'd leave that up to Santa.

The rest of the afternoon was perfect. They stopped by the independent bookstore, A Book for All Seasons, and Lindy bought an autographed copy by one of her favorite authors. Their next stop was the cheese store, and Billy picked up Brie from France to contribute to his sister's Christmas dinner.

"Will you spend Christmas with Dede?" She assumed the restaurant would be closed on Christmas Day.

"That's the plan for now."

For now? He made it sound as if there might be a change in his plans. It made her wonder if he'd made other arrangements with another woman. A tinge of curiosity niggled in her mind until she reminded herself it shouldn't matter. She would be returning to Seattle after the first of the year. This time together was a pleasant interlude and one her self-esteem badly needed, but they were both fully aware her time in Wenatchee was limited.

As they strolled along the way, the crowds swirled around them: the noise, laughter, and music, all part of the enchantment.

There was no shortage of interesting shops to visit, and before long it was time for their dinner reservation at Berghoff's. They walked to the restaurant, hand in hand to keep them from being separated in the mingling crowd. Whatever the reason, Lindy enjoyed being linked to him.

The line into the restaurant progressed along, and soon they were at the check-in. The hostess collected their coats and led them across the room. As expected, every table was occupied, and the restaurant was hopping. A fire blazed from the rock-hewn fireplace, warming the room. Soft lighting created a cozy, if not romantic, atmosphere.

Once seated, they were handed menus. When their server appeared, Billy ordered a wine from a local winery, and within a short amount of time it was delivered to their table.

"Dan will be right over," the server told Billy.

"Dan is the owner," Billy explained. "He's been a mentor to me for the last couple of years, plus being a good friend."

"I look forward to meeting him." Eating at Berghoff's was a rare treat. Her family had never been able to get reservations, and Lindy hadn't mentioned where Billy was taking her, in case it fell through at the last minute.

"Dan has relatives in Chicago," Billy explained. "Their restaurant was one of the most notable in the city for any number of years. I had another restaurant in Yakima before coming to Wenatchee. Dan was instrumental in advising me when I came to him about opening the Wine Press. His family has been in the business for years. I appreciated his advice."

Lindy vaguely remembered hearing about the relationship between the Chicago restaurant and the one in Leavenworth, some years ago, while in college.

"What happened to your restaurant in Yakima?" Lindy asked, wondering if he was managing more than the one in Wenatchee.

He didn't answer right away, and looked relieved when Dan approached their table, leaving her to wonder what had happened in Yakima, as he didn't seem to want to discuss it.

"Will, good to see you," Dan said, as he stepped closer. Billy stood, and the two men briefly hugged. "Appreciate you squeezing us in tonight," he said.

The restaurant owner was around fifty, if Lindy were to guess. He had a thick head of salt-and-pepper hair, warm blue eyes, and a well-trimmed beard. His smile was personable.

"Wednesday night wasn't a huge problem. The weekend would have been impossible." He reached for the wine bottle and opened it with an expert hand. He glanced toward Lindy.

Billy reached across the table and took her hand. "This is Lindy, the woman I mentioned earlier."

"Ah yes," Dan said, his gaze welcoming, revealing a bit of intrigue, as if he knew something she didn't. "It's a pleasure, Lindy."

"It's nice to meet you, and again, thank you for finding us a table for tonight."

"My joy, sweet lady."

Billy leaned forward, pressing his midsection against the table. In a stage whisper, he said, "I didn't tell him about your letter to Santa."

"What's this about a letter?" Dan pried.

"What would you recommend off the menu?" Lindy asked, gently kicking Billy under the table.

"Ouch," he cried, pretending she'd mortally wounded him. "It's nothing," he told his friend, and then added in another stage whisper, "I'll tell you later."

Dan laughed and turned his attention to Lindy. "I highly recommend the rouladen and the spätzle with purple cabbage. It's one of our signature dishes. You can't go wrong."

"I've heard of spätzle, but not rouladen."

"It's thinly sliced beef, layered with bacon and sliced onion, and then rolled around a thick slice of pickle. Trust me, Lindy, you won't be disappointed."

"Then that's what I'll have."

Lindy did well to have taken Dan's word, as the dinner was everything she'd hoped it would be. They lingered over a dessert called donauwelle. Dan explained that it was basically pound cake flavored with vanilla. Then the top was filled with cherries, a thick layer of buttercream, along with a thin covering of chocolate ganache. Every bite was pure heaven. The meal was finished with a cup of decaf coffee.

Dan escorted them to the door once they were ready to leave and handed them their coats. He took Lindy's hand and kissed it. "Meeting you was a delight," he said.

"Hey, buddy," Billy teased, "that's my girl."

His girl! Lindy couldn't have hidden her smile if she'd tried.

"The French side of his family comes out every now and again," Billy said, as he placed his arm around Lindy's waist and steered her out the back entrance, where he'd parked the truck.

Billy helped her inside, then walked around the front. Once inside, he started the engine and let it warm up enough to clear the frost off the windshield.

"I had the most marvelous day," Lindy told him, and it

was the truth. Every aspect of their afternoon and evening had been simply wonderful. Even seeing Brian with Celeste hadn't hampered her time. This day would be one she long treasured.

"I don't want it to end," Billy said.

"I don't, either."

"Good. Let's stop off at the Wine Press. There's a special ice wine I'd like you to taste. It's a favorite of mine, and I think you'll enjoy it, too."

Ice wine would be a treat. The grapes could be harvested only in climates where temperatures dropped to below freezing. The grapes were kept on the vine to sweeten until the first frost of the season. They were then handpicked, generally in the dark of night, after the grapes had frozen. The excessively sweet wine wasn't to everyone's taste. Lindy happened to like it. The bottles were narrow and thin, and often expensive, due to the labor costs.

"I'd like that," she said.

"It'll give me a chance to check in with the night manager, too. It might be my day off, but I make a habit of checking in at some point during the day."

The responsibility of being an owner/operator must weigh heavily on Billy. It told her he didn't likely have time for a relationship, not with him working six days a week. Even on his day off, he ran interference. The restaurant was constantly on his mind, as it should be. Billy understood this could be only a holiday romance. She was of the same mind.

Even though it was after eight, the restaurant was busy; every seat at the bar was taken. Billy secured a table and left Lindy while he went to check in with the manager. When he returned, he had the bottle of ice wine and two special glasses that resembled miniature wineglasses.

He sat next to her and poured them each a small amount. "A little goes a long way with ice wine," he said. Again, the wine was one from Washington State. Only northern climates had the necessary temperatures cold enough to produce ice wine.

"The Toronto area has some wonderful ice wines as well," he said, as he gently clinked his glass against hers.

"What shall we toast?" Lindy asked.

"How about we toast to Santa."

Lindy laughed. "To Santa," she said, and raised the glass to her lips.

The wine was extrasweet, and cold. It tasted a bit like honey and came to life in her mouth. She smiled to herself, thinking this was like a cavity in a glass.

"Do you like it?" Billy asked.

"It's wonderful." It was the perfect complement to their magical day.

CHAPTER TEN

Lindy's mom watched Peter every Thursday, so Lindy was able to spend the morning with her precious nephew. He was a ball of fire. This precocious four-year-old had wrapped his way around her heart from the day he'd been born.

Chad's wife worked at a small arts-and-crafts store owned by her parents. Now that Ashley was pregnant, she worked part-time, helping her parents out two days a week. Because Lindy's mother had them for dinner on Thursday nights, that was the day she also kept Peter. After a long day on her feet, Ashley appreciated not needing to rush home and prepare dinner. Lindy's mother was thoughtful that way.

For this evening, her mother had a Mississippi pot

roast simmering in the Crock-Pot, which, Lindy knew, was one of Chad's favorites. After spending the morning entertaining Peter with Beau's help, Lindy got Peter down for his nap. He resisted until she promised him a sledding trip in the park after Christmas. Once she was sure he was asleep, she slipped away to meet Peggy for lunch.

Following their food scavenger hunt, when Peggy learned Lindy would be spending Wednesday afternoon with Billy, she'd insisted they meet so she could hear all the details. Lindy had stopped by Peggy's office earlier and solved a minor back-end website problem. Peggy used that excuse to pay for Lindy's lunch, but Lindy knew it was more to drill her about her day with Billy. Lindy had agreed, mainly because any time spent with Peggy was sure to be fun.

Lindy parked and noticed that her friend had already arrived and was seated in a booth by the window in the fifties-style diner, known as the Big Apple Diner. Even knowing she was about to undergo an inquisition, Lindy was happy to see Peggy.

She slid into the booth. "Hey, girl," she said, as she reached for the menu, which was tucked behind the old-style jukebox.

"Hey, yourself," Peggy greeted. "So, don't keep me in suspense, how was your date with Billy the Kid?"

"Can I look at the menu first?" Lindy teased.

"No. I've only got an hour; I've already ordered for us. I want details."

"What did you order?"

"Cobb salads for us both. Now spill." She cocked her head to one side and grinned shrewdly, as if seeing Lindy's smile told her everything she needed to know.

"What?" Lindy asked, as a saucy grin spread over Peggy's beautiful face.

She shrugged. "You don't need to say a word, I can see everything was super just by your look."

"You're full of it." Lindy immediately lowered her gaze, afraid of what her friend saw in her.

"I know what I know. You can deny all you want. Tell me everything, and don't leave out the juicy details." Peggy was relentless.

"Peggy!"

"Did he—"

Lindy wagged her index finger. "I'm not one to kiss and tell."

"Ah, so there was kissing." Peggy jiggled her eyebrows suggestively.

"All right, I'll admit it was a fabulously fun day." The truth was, that afternoon and evening with Billy had been the best time Lindy could remember in a very long while.

"When are the two of you getting together next?"

Her nosy friend wasn't going to drop this until she got the details she wanted.

"He did ask you out again, didn't he?"

"No, he didn't." Lindy neglected to mention how busy the Christmas holidays were for the restaurant. Companies had booked office parties, and every available table was reserved until Christmas and into the week that followed. It went without Billy needing to explain, although he had, that he couldn't take time off until after Christmas, other than a few odd hours here and there. But he'd encouraged Lindy to stop by anytime.

Peggy looked insulted. "You mean to tell me Billy wined and dined you and let it go at that?"

"Yes. You're putting more into this than warranted. Billy was thanking me for my help, is all." No way was she mentioning the kiss they'd shared on the sleigh ride or the ones after he drove her home. That was private.

Because Peggy insisted, Lindy caved and filled her in on her day with Billy, the sleigh ride, and especially the dinner. Other than the kiss, she left out running into Celeste and Brian. She might have said something if Peggy hadn't been so full of questions. Lindy had barely answered one and her friend fired off another, wanting in on every small detail.

When she'd finished, Peggy said, with that same I-know-you-better-than-you-think look, "You like Billy. Don't bother to deny it."

"Really?"

"Yes, really. It's obvious he feels the same way about you. Anyone with half a brain can see the two of you have chemistry." She raised both hands and made explosion signs.

"You mean like Romeo and Juliet?" she teased. "Bogie and Bacall?"

"You think I'm joking. I saw the way you two looked at each other the other night. It's sweet and makes me wish there was a man in my life." She heaved a sigh loud enough to make Lindy laugh out loud.

The server delivered their salads. After all the indulgences of the day before, Lindy ate sparingly. Peggy was both tall and thin, and seemed not to worry about calories. Lindy envied her friend's ability to eat any- and everything and still maintain her trim figure.

"You showed me your pictures from high school. How is it you weigh the same now as you did then?" Lindy asked.

Peggy shrugged. "Good genes."

"Well, I have skinny jeans and they won't fit if I continue to eat like I did yesterday." She mentioned the dessert she'd had after the German dinner and how decadent it was.

"That sounds delicious."

"It was."

Peggy's gaze narrowed. "You're changing the subject."

"Not on purpose. I had a great time with Billy, but that's as far as it goes. Remember, I'm in town only until after New Year's, and then I need to return to Seattle. Billy knows that, too. Whatever this is can last these two weeks and no longer."

"Do you have to go back to Seattle?" Peggy pushed out her bottom lip in a pout with the question.

The question caught Lindy up short. She hadn't given moving back to Wenatchee a thought. To her surprise, she was immediately drawn to the idea. Reconnecting with Peggy and Billy, too, held a lot of appeal. As quickly as the thought came, reality set in. If her proposal was accepted, there was no way she could leave Media Blast, not after the hours and effort that had gone into the project.

"It's a good thought," she said, "but my life is in Seattle. I'm six months into a year lease on my apartment. I can't up and move now, even if I wanted. Besides, I have a great job."

"Didn't you tell me how underappreciated you are?"

That was true. Still, Lindy was determined to prove herself, and she hoped this latest proposal would do it.

"I've been thinking," Peggy said, growing serious. "I looked at what you did for Billy's website and, Lindy, it's fabulous. Have you ever thought about doing freelance work?"

She hadn't, and shook her head.

"I know several businesses that would like to have updated websites. You'd fill a real need."

"I can't do that, Peggy, not when I work for Media Blast."

"Then don't work for them. Move back to Wenatchee and go out on your own. Without a doubt you'd be a success."

That would be a Jack-and-the-Beanstalk giant leap of faith, and not one Lindy was willing to take. "I don't have the connections to do that."

"But I do. I can help; I have lots of connections," Peggy told her, as if what she suggested was a small thing. Lindy would be risking everything.

Lindy shook her head. "Sorry . . . Maybe sometime down the road."

Peggy reluctantly accepted her decision.

Once her lunch hour was over, Peggy returned to the office, and Lindy picked up a few items her mother had asked her to collect for dinner. She was walking into the house when her phone dinged.

It was a text from Billy.

Found your glove in the truck. You home?

Yes.

See you in a few.

This was an unexpected surprise. She'd missed the red glove when she'd left to meet Peggy. The only place it could be was in Billy's truck. She meant to ask him about it but had decided to wait until later. She would have saved him the trouble and collected it herself. Seeing that he wanted to deliver it himself was even better.

"You're back," Peter said, running as fast as his legs could carry him as soon as she walked in the door. Beau barked his greeting and raced alongside Peter. Whenever she returned, Beau acted like she'd been gone forever and he'd been anxiously waiting for her to come home so she would pet him.

Setting aside her purse and the grocery bag, Lindy hauled her nephew into her arms. "Did you have a good nap?"

Peter nodded enthusiastically.

"You wore him out this morning," her mother said, from the kitchen.

"Billy's on his way over," she said, as she headed into her bedroom. Peter and Beau tagged behind her.

"Who's Billy?" Peter asked.

"A friend."

"Does he like playing in the snow?"

Lindy shrugged. "I don't know, you'll have to ask him yourself."

"Okay."

Wanting to make sure she looked her best for Billy, Lindy touched up her makeup and ran a flat iron through her hair. She was applying lip gloss when the doorbell chimed. She let her mother and Peter answer the door. Right away she heard Peter asking Billy if he would go sledding with them for fun in the snow. Lindy rolled her eyes. Oh dear. She hadn't meant for that to happen. She'd explain it to Billy later.

Inhaling a deep breath, Lindy centered herself. It would be far and away too easy to let her heart get ahead of her brain when it came to Billy. She couldn't let that happen. This was a temporary situation. A Christmas romance, and it would end when she left Wenatchee. Billy had a business to run. She wasn't going to encourage anything beyond the two weeks she was in town.

By the time she appeared, her mother had brought Billy into the kitchen. He sat at the kitchen table. Her mother had poured him coffee and was gathering cookies for a plate. Peter was munching on a cookie as he sat on the family room floor watching *Paw Patrol,* his favorite cartoon series. Ever attentive, Beau was at his side.

"Ah, here's Lindy."

"Hey," she said, a little self-conscious. She wasn't sure why, other than the fact that her mother was in the room.

"Hey," he returned.

Their eyes locked, and it felt as if they'd been apart years instead of a few hours. Her heart seemed to roar inside her chest, as if looking to make a break for it.

"I have your glove," he said, and the way he said the words made it sound as if he held her heart in the palm of his hand. Lindy was afraid he just might, and that was dangerous for a wide variety of reasons.

She remembered removing her glove when they'd kissed inside his truck. The need to bury her fingers in the hair at the base of his neck had been too much to resist. She'd torn off her gloves and stuffed them into her coat pocket. Apparently, only one of them had made it inside. The look they shared assured her that Billy remembered exactly when she'd removed it as keenly as she did.

"There must be a lull at the restaurant," she said, making a determined effort to break eye contact.

He nodded.

Her mother delivered the cookies to the table and then returned to whatever it was she was doing.

"Whatever you're cooking, Mrs. Carmichael, smells delicious."

"Chad and Ashley are coming for dinner," Lindy explained. "Mississippi pot roast is my brother's favorite."

"Never heard of it."

"It's made with pepperoncinis," Ellen explained, as she set the lid back on the Crock-Pot.

"Never thought of them having anything to do with Mississippi," Billy said.

Lindy had to agree. She didn't know how the dish got its name. "Come to think of it, me neither."

"Billy, why don't you join us for dinner?" her mother offered, turning to face them. "We'd love to have you."

Billy looked to Lindy, as if seeking her reaction.

"Could you get away?" Lindy hoped it was possible. The last thing she wanted was to put pressure on him, knowing how busy the restaurant would be this evening.

"We'll eat around six," her mother added.

Billy reached for Lindy's hand and gave it a quick squeeze. "I could get away for an hour, I suppose. I've been there since eight this morning. I could use a break."

Lindy hadn't dared to hope he would take the time away, and squeezed his hand back. "That's great." And then, because she didn't want him to feel an obligation on her behalf, she added, "Are you sure?"

"Positive. The restaurant has taken over my life. I need to make time for myself now and again," he said, and added in a whisper so low she wasn't sure she heard correctly, "Time for us."

"What about Christmas?" she asked, feeling brave. "I know you said you were spending it with your sister, but do you think you might be able to stop by here?"

"I'd like that."

"That'd be great." She couldn't hide the joy she felt knowing she would spend part of the day with him.

"I don't suppose you know anyone willing to play Santa," her mother asked, lowering her voice so Peter wouldn't hear.

"I do," Billy said.

"This is the first year Peter's into Santa. I'd love it if Santa could stop by the house at some point on Christmas Day. I know it's a lot to ask of a stranger, but I'd be willing to pay whatever was reasonable."

"I doubt he'd take the money. I know for a fact he'd refuse."

"Who is it?" Ellen asked.

Billy's smile was huge. "You're looking at him. I have a Santa suit and play Santa for Dede's kids. I got the suit last year and have already made an appearance for an office party at the restaurant."

"Billy Kincade," Lindy said, with laughter in her voice. "You are a man of many talents. What other hidden qualities do you have?"

His gaze sparkled, and he lowered his voice and said, "So many. I'll be happy to show you them all one day."

Lindy laughed. "I'll look forward to that."

His phone dinged, and he removed it from his pocket and sighed when he read the message. "I need to get back to the restaurant."

"I'll walk you to the door," Lindy offered.

Her mother pretended to be busy in the kitchen, and Lindy let her. Billy held her hand, and once they were in the other room, he gathered her in his arms. "I can't stop thinking about you, Lindy. When I found your glove, I was excited because it gave me the perfect excuse to see you again."

"You don't need an excuse, Billy."

His intense gaze held hers.

"I have the strongest urge to kiss you."

Lindy briefly closed her eyes, remembering their ardent kisses from the night before. "And I have the strongest urge to let you."

Billy brought his mouth to hers in a gentle kiss that Lindy felt all the way to the bottom of her feet. Her arms circled his middle as she leaned up on her tiptoes, holding herself against him. He tasted like ginger from the cookie he'd eaten earlier. She'd never enjoyed the taste more. When they broke apart, he continued to hold her, his forehead against the top of her head.

"Tell me I'm not alone in this feeling, Lindy. I need to hear you say it."

"You aren't alone."

She heard his sigh, of what must be relief. Even though she'd repeatedly told herself this was a holiday romance, it felt like it was more and that was dangerous. Dangerous for her, and dangerous for Billy, too. When her vacation time was up, she would return to Seattle. She needed to remind Billy of that.

Not now, though.

CHAPTER ELEVEN

When Chad and Ashley arrived, Peter hurried to his parents to tell them about his day. He didn't fail to mention that Lindy had promised to take him to play in the snow after Christmas.

"You're a brave woman," her brother told her.

"I want Billy to come, too," Peter added.

Chad's brows lifted in question. "Peter invited him," she said. Although she hoped he would be able to join them, it all depended on his schedule.

With Chad, Ashley, and Peter there, the house was filled with excited chatter about their day and plans for Christmas. Taking hold of Lindy's hand, Peter brought her over to the nativity her mother had set up on the table by the tree. He stood with wide eyes in front of the figures displayed there.

"I don't know why the baby Jesus had to sleep in the hay."

"Because there was no room for his mom and dad at the inn," Lindy explained.

"Was it cold in the barn?" he asked.

"I'm sure it was warm for Him and his mom and dad."

"Good."

That appeared to appease Peter.

"Aunt Lindy," Peter said, holding on to her hand. "Did you know Santa is coming to our house?"

"Did you write him a letter to tell him what you wanted for Christmas?" she asked, enjoying the way he looked up at her, his sweet, innocent face filled with the excitement of the holidays.

"I don't write good yet. But I can write my name."

"I saw that and was impressed. You're growing up so fast."

"I like school."

Lindy knew Peter attended a preschool three days a week, and was amazed with all he was learning. It seemed every week her young nephew blew her away with some new accomplishment.

"Did you have fun with the paper-chain set I mailed you?" she asked.

"Lindy, that was the best," Ashley told her, joining

them. Six months into the pregnancy, she was starting to show a little more every day. It'd been the same with Peter. Ashley didn't begin to look pregnant until the end of her seventh month. If she were ever to have children, Lindy hoped . . . Her thoughts came to an abrupt halt. She couldn't imagine where these ideas were coming from. Children? Her?

"Peter and Chad put together that paper chain in no time."

"We put it on the Christmas tree," Peter said. "It's pretty."

Lindy had found the paper-chain kit in a catalog and ordered it for Peter, knowing how much he'd enjoy it.

At six, when her mother set dinner on the table, Billy had yet to show. Ellen looked to Lindy, as if to seek her advice.

"Should we wait?" she asked.

Before she could answer, the doorbell rang. Billy had arrived.

Lindy was surprised with how well Billy fit in with her family, especially her dad. It was as if he'd been part of their Christmas traditions for years. Chad and Ashley and Peter planned to spend Christmas Eve with Ashey's parents. The two families traded off the holidays. This year it was the Carmichaels' turn for Christmas Day. Christmas morning was reserved for Chad and Ashley and young

Peter to set their own family traditions. Then, in the afternoon, they would come for dinner and the gift exchange.

Lindy knew it was a delicate balance when in-laws became involved. She admired her parents, who along with Ashley's had come up with a workable plan so neither family felt as if they were being slighted.

Chad and Billy chatted away like long-lost friends. It pleased Lindy how accepting her family was of him. Lindy sat next to Billy at the table. He reached for her hand and gave her fingers a gentle squeeze as if to say how pleased he was to be with her.

Naturally, the topic of her childhood letter to Santa arose, and Lindy was the subject of a lot of teasing. Seeing how much she enjoyed being with Billy, she took the joking in stride, laughing along with them.

The hour flew past as if it were only minutes, and all too soon Billy rose, declining dessert. Lindy walked him to the door. With his touch at her elbow, Billy gently pulled her outside and wrapped her in his arms to kiss her. She could easily grow accustomed to Billy's kisses. If she remained in town much longer, she feared they would quickly become addictive.

Once again, she reminded herself whatever this attraction was between them wasn't meant to last. With every passing day she struggled to remember this could be only a holiday fling. Every time Billy kissed her, however, it became harder to hold on to that resolve.

"Can you stop by the restaurant later?" he asked, knotting his hands at the small of her back and looking down on her.

With his eyes full of warmth and hope, she found it difficult to refuse him. "You're going to be busy, maybe—"

"It's always busy. I'll find time to steal away, even if it's just for a few minutes."

Lindy gave in for the simple reason that she wanted to spend time with him, however long he could spare. "I probably won't be able to get away until after ten."

"Anytime. I'll take what I can get."

Lindy felt the same. Whatever few minutes he had to spare would be worth the hassle. She'd help her mother with cleanup and spend as much time with Chad, Ashley, and Peter as she could. Because Peter would need to go to bed at a decent hour, she suspected they wouldn't stay much later than nine.

Once Billy left, Lindy helped her mother clear the table and dealt with the leftovers. Peter was vying for her attention as she started stacking dishes in the washer. Her mother shooed her out of the kitchen to entertain Peter.

Her nephew was a precious little boy, curious and eager to learn and grow. Smart, too. The range of his vocabulary shocked her.

"Can you come live with us, Aunt Lindy?" he asked, as he sat at her side with a book in his hand.

"I live in Seattle, remember?"

"But couldn't you move here?"

"My apartment is there," she explained patiently.

"You could get an apartment here," he said, reasoning with her with his head tilted back to look up at her. His dark brown eyes implored her.

"My job is there, too. I go to work each day just like your mom and dad. There are people who would miss me if I left." How Lindy wished that were true, although she suspected her coworkers at Media Blast wouldn't.

Peter sighed and leaned his head against the side of her arm. "You could work here. Daddy works here, and Mommy, too."

Rather than go into details and lengthy explanations, Lindy opened the book. "Maybe someday," she said, hoping that would satisfy her sweet nephew.

"When Mommy says 'someday,' that means no," he said with a pout.

Lindy laughed. The kid was smarter than she gave him credit. "Are you ready for the story?" she asked, hoping to change the subject.

"Okay."

The story was one Lindy had from her own childhood, about the donkey in the stable who stood guard over the manger. The much-loved book was held together with duct tape on the binding. As she read the story, she glanced down at Peter and watched as his eyes slowly drifted closed, even while he fought to stay awake. By the time she finished the last page, he was slouched against her side and sound asleep.

Chad sat down on the ottoman in front of Lindy. "Tell me about you and Billy," he said, not bothering to ease into the subject.

"What's there to tell? We connected and I'm enjoying his company."

"Are you two serious?"

Lindy laughed off the question. "No. We're having fun together while I'm home. That's it."

"You sure about that? I saw him watching you at dinner, and sis, I have to tell you, he had the look."

"The look?" Chad had to be joking. Sure, she'd spent time with Billy, more with him than anyone else—well, other than her parents and Peggy. She'd been home less than a week, and that was far too soon for "the look."

"Be careful," Chad advised, his eyes growing serious.

"I think you're imagining things, little brother. Billy is far too preoccupied with his restaurant. He knows I'm in town only until the first of the year."

"I'm not worried about Billy," her brother said. "My concern is for you."

"Me?" she asked with a slight laugh, finding his observation just short of hilarious.

"Yes, you. I saw how Billy looked at you, but I also noticed the way you looked at him, and it was telling. I know how upset you were over Brian and Celeste. I never said anything, but I was never keen on Brian. I figured in time he'd show his true colors, and he did. I will say this, though, I like Billy. I don't think you'd be wrong to consider a more permanent relationship with him."

Her brother's words gave Lindy pause. Perhaps he was right and she was setting herself up for more heartache. She assumed she'd learned her lesson. This thing with Billy had started out as . . . what? She couldn't be sure. It went all the way back to her letter to Santa all those years ago.

Something powerful had happened the day they'd spent in Leavenworth. The sleigh ride, sitting on Santa's lap . . . the kisses.

Oh yes, those kisses.

"Hey," Chad said, interrupting her musings. "I didn't upset you, did I?"

"No, you gave me something to think about. The thing is, I have no intention of getting seriously involved with Billy. It wouldn't work, for all the reasons I've already mentioned."

"That's too bad, because the two of you are good together."

Ashley came to stand beside Chad, with one hand rubbing the slight mound of her tummy. "It's time we head out," she said. "I hate to go, but Peter needs his sleep, and for that matter, so do I. We've got two busy days ahead of us."

Chad stood and gently lifted his son from the chair. Ashley, careful not to wake the sleeping boy, placed his arms in his winter coat. Lindy's parents helped usher them out the door while confirming the time they planned to arrive on Christmas Day.

Her mother had spent the afternoon cooking, and yawned as she returned to the house.

"Sit down, Mom," Lindy urged. "Relax. Let me get you a cup of peppermint tea."

"Thank you, sweetie." Ellen didn't argue as she sat in her favorite chair in the family room and reached for her knitting.

All too soon her parents were both settled in front of the television, and Lindy knew this was the best time for her to leave to see Billy.

"I'm going to head out for a little bit," she said.

Her father nodded, as if it was what he expected. "We like Billy," he said, letting her know without saying it that he knew where she was headed.

Dressed in her coat and gloves, she felt she needed to clarify the situation. "We aren't serious."

Both her parents looked away from the television at the same time and focused their eyes directly on her. Neither said anything. No need, their expressions said it all. It felt like the two of them, along with Chad, had insider information she had yet to receive.

With all the verbal and nonverbal warnings given to her this evening, Lindy should probably avoid Billy. She toyed with sending a text and making an excuse. That seemed wrong, after she'd already agreed. Once in her car and on her way to the Wine Press, Lindy admitted she wanted to be with Billy, and to tell herself otherwise would be a lie.

The parking lot was full when she arrived. That likely meant Billy would be unable to sneak away even for a limited amount of time. Which should be enough to discourage her, only it wasn't.

Entering the lounge, she found him behind the bar with another bartender, filling orders with an expert hand. When he saw her, he smiled and said something to the other bartender.

Lindy found an empty seat and sat while she patiently waited for Billy. Within a few minutes one of the servers stepped behind the bar and Billy made his way to her.

"Busy night," she said, stating the obvious.

"Very. It'll slow down after the first of the year, when the credit-card statements hit the mail and reality sets in."

So true. Lindy remembered last Christmas when she saw the balance on her own credit card. It was ramen noodles for dinner for the entire month.

"You should take care of business," she said, looking at the crowded room and how busy the bar section was. "We can connect tomorrow."

Billy intertwined their fingers and shook his head. "I don't care how busy we are. I don't want you to leave."

His words made a direct hit to her heart—bull's-eye. Right away her brother's warning took root. It was time she owned up to the fact that she was seriously in danger of falling for Billy Kincade.

"What are your plans for tomorrow?" he asked.

Her mind was mush. It took her a long moment before she was able to respond. "Peggy phoned before dinner with some crazy scheme she wouldn't tell me over the phone. I'm meeting her for coffee. Then there's the Christmas Eve church service with Mom and Dad."

"Do you think you could squeeze me in?"

Feeling as if she was getting in over her head, she should make an excuse and tell him her day was already full. She didn't, though. So much for her resolve! Instead, she nodded, knowing she wouldn't deny him and at the same time herself.

"Give me thirty minutes and I'll be back." He slid off the seat and kissed her forehead.

"Okay."

He left, and within a couple minutes a server brought a glass of red wine to her table. While waiting, she watched the bar crowd and noticed a large party was calling for their tab. After they left, the bar area quieted down, and Lindy was able to hear the Christmas music for the first time.

As soon as the door closed on the group, Billy joined her. He looked dead on his feet, with little wonder. He was at the restaurant long before it opened and then late into the night. Those kinds of hours would drain anyone's energy. She wished there were something she could do to ease his work schedule.

"I wanted to tell you all the compliments I've gotten on the website," he said, as he relaxed in the seat, sitting beside her.

"That's great."

"A couple friends asked me who designed it. I won't pass along your name unless you want me to."

She shook her head. "I won't be in town long enough. Sorry."

Billy took hold of her hand and gazed down at it, as if something were written there that he needed to decipher. "You're returning to Seattle?" He made it into a question.

"Of course. It's where I live and work."

He nodded, as if needing the reminder.

Not wanting the conversation to wander down this road, she changed the subject. "What's your Christmas going to be like?" she asked, brightly, perhaps a bit too cheerfully.

Billy took the hint. "I'll spend it with my sister and her family. Your mom gave me the time to stop by in my Santa costume for Peter and that's about it."

"What about your mother?"

His eyes grew sad. "She died three years ago."

"Oh, Billy, I'm sorry, I didn't know."

He accepted her condolence. "She never remarried, worked all her life, and just when she was to a point where she could enjoy a bit of leisure time, she came down with this virus that went into her lungs. It was quick. Before we had a chance to realize how serious it was, she was gone."

"Have you had contact with your dad over the years?" It was a personal question and one he might not want to answer. "I shouldn't have asked that."

Billy squeezed her fingers; Lindy doubted he was aware he had. It appeared to be a jerk reaction to her mentioning his father. "Dad remarried after he left us that Christmas and started a new family. It was like he wanted to start over. Mom, Dede, and I were part of a past he wiped from his memory. It was as if we no longer existed. Dede reached out to him a couple times, and he made sure she knew it wasn't appreciated."

Hearing this made Lindy want to cry. "What a snake," she said, angry on Billy's behalf.

"He's gone as well. He died in a boating accident on the Columbia River. Another boat slammed into his and his boat sank. His body was recovered several days later. Mom heard about it on the news and told Dede and me."

Lindy had little sympathy for the man who had wreaked havoc in young Billy's life.

"The thing is," Billy said, still looking down at her hand, which was swallowed up in his much larger one, "he did us a favor by leaving. It didn't seem that way at the time. It felt as if our entire world imploded. We moved in with my grandparents for a while and then later into a tiny apartment while Mom worked two jobs. Both Dede and I had to grow up fast. We learned the value of hard work and a deep appreciation for what we had. We lived in terror of him and his dark moods when he was home. The truth is, we were better off without him."

Lindy agreed and was forever grateful for the love and strong relationship her parents shared. This same tenderness and concern were what she hoped to find in her own life partner.

Lindy noticed that the bar was as busy as it had been earlier. Billy needed to get back to work.

"I'm headed home. What time should I stop by tomorrow?" she asked.

"Anytime. I'll be around all day."

"You aren't closing for Christmas Eve?"

He shook his head. "We're booked solid the entire day."

She sensed he would have liked to close early, not only for himself but for his staff. Turning away business would be difficult, especially when he was still getting his feet under him financially.

"I'll walk you to your car."

"Billy, it's okay. You're busy."

"Not too busy to see you safely to your car," he insisted.

When they started outside, Lindy noticed a light snowfall. "I do so love it when it snows this close to Christmas," she said, looking up at the sky and the flakes slowly drifting down to cover the landscape.

Billy opened her car door for her, and after she was safely tucked inside, he leaned down and kissed her. "Sleep well."

"You, too," she whispered.

Billy stood in the parking lot, snow gently swirling around him as she eased onto the street to drive back to her parents' house.

As she pulled into the driveway of the family home, her phone rang. She reached for it and hesitated when she saw the name on the screen. It rang a second and a third time before she found the courage to answer.

"Hello, Celeste," she said, keeping her voice cool and calm.

CHAPTER TWELVE

"Merry Christmas," Celeste greeted hesitantly.

She said it as if they were still the best of friends. As if when Lindy had learned the truth about her and Brian, it had been nothing more than a friendly exchange of insignificant differences. Billy had been with her when she'd run into them at Leavenworth. Having him at her side had given her confidence.

Lindy remained silent. She would have spoken, if she'd been able to find the words, but none came.

Pretending not to notice, Celeste continued, as if Lindy had welcomed the sound of her voice. "Are you with your family?"

"Yes," she somehow managed . . . She remembered the pastor's sermon from last Sunday. Forgiveness had been the theme. Lindy had walked out of the service and felt free, as though a huge burden had been lifted from her shoulders. Now that she was speaking to the friend who had betrayed her, she wasn't sure how she should react.

"Yeah, me, too," Celeste continued. "Christmas is for families, right?"

"Right." Lindy noticed she didn't mention Brian. She wouldn't ask, though.

"Brian is with his mother," Celeste continued, as if she felt it was necessary to let Lindy know.

That made sense, since Brian's parents had divorced when he was in high school and his mother lived alone. Brian chose to champion his mother and refused to reconcile with his father. From what he'd told her, he hadn't had any contact with his dad in years.

Lindy wasn't sure what more she could say, other than to ask why Celeste had called, especially this late at night. "I'm not sure why you phoned," Lindy said. It had to be more than to tell Lindy that she and Brian weren't together for Christmas.

The awkward silence that followed made Lindy uncomfortable. Celeste had been her best friend for ten years. They'd shared confidences, clothes, had been roommates, and as close as sisters. It was one thing to lose Brian, probably inevitable, in hindsight. The bigger loss was Celeste. In her view, a best friend was much harder to replace.

"Brian and I were surprised when we saw you in Leavenworth. I wanted to say more then, I really did, only I didn't know what."

Lindy understood, as she'd been shocked when she first caught sight of them as well. She'd had time during the sleigh ride to recover. Celeste had been taken completely by surprise and was speechless.

"You looked great, and the guy you were with was a hunk."

"I knew Billy when I was in grade school," Lindy said.

"You looked happy."

"I am happy," she said with all sincerity.

"I'm glad. That makes me feel better."

"Listen, Celeste, I don't know why you called, but I'm grateful you did."

"You are?" She sounded unsure, apprehensive, as if expecting a tongue-lashing.

"Yes, because I want you and Brian to know you deeply wounded me. I carried that hurt with me like an aching sore until I realized the only way to heal that pain was to forgive you both and move on. That's what I'm doing. I wish you and Brian the best, and I sincerely mean that. So Merry Christmas, Celeste. And thank you for calling."

"Wait . . ." Celeste pleaded. "It's taken half a bottle of

wine for me to find the courage to call you. Please let me say this one thing."

Although Lindy was anxious to get off the phone, she agreed. "Okay."

"I'm so sorry, Lindy. I should have told you about Brian and me. I meant to, I sincerely did. I hated the way you found out we were together. We should have told you long before you stopped off at the apartment."

Celeste clearly had no idea of what a shock it had been to find the two of them together. "Listen, if you're looking for absolution, you have it. Life goes on. I should have realized sooner what was happening." As painful as it was to admit, that was the truth. "It was right in front of my eyes, and I couldn't see it." In the aftermath of her discovery, Lindy wanted to kick herself for being so blind and trusting. She was foolish to ignore what should have been obvious.

"I . . . don't deserve your forgiveness," Celeste said.

"I did it for myself. The anger wasn't doing me any good." It was clear Celeste was dealing with a massive bout of guilt.

"Thank you," she whispered. "I'm so sorry, Lindy. Really, really sorry."

Lindy believed her regret was real. How good it felt to tell Celeste that she was forgiven and to mean it. "I accept your apology. Now it's time to move on."

"One more thing," Celeste rushed to add. "I need to say one more thing before we hang up."

"Okay."

"You're the best friend I ever had, and I mean that with all my heart. I realize our friendship will never be the same, and I accept the blame for that. But I hope someday in the future that we might be able to reconnect."

"Time will tell." Lindy said.

"Time is a great healer, right? I mean, that's something my mother always says. And, Lindy, I want you to know something. You're talented and smart, and whatever you do will be a success."

"Thank you," Lindy said, feeling lighter than she had in a long while.

"Okay," Celeste said. "I've said everything I wanted to tell you. Bye, Lindy."

"Bye, Celeste."

The house was quiet when Lindy went inside. Her parents had already gone to bed. Her head was reeling from the conversation with Celeste. She doubted she'd be able to sleep. She headed into her room and readied for bed, dressing in her flannel pj's, unaccustomed to these bitterly cold nights. Fluffing the pillow, she sat up and reached for her phone, scrolling through Facebook and then playing a few online games. She'd crushed Candy Crush and had moved on to another game, realizing that all she was doing was killing time until she was too tired to function any longer. On a whim she sent Peggy a text.

You awake?

When her friend didn't respond, Lindy figured Peggy was dead to the world, and rightly so. It was after one. Anyone with a working brain was asleep by this time of night. Unless Billy was still up. She hesitated, and then sent him a text on the off chance he was still awake.

You home yet?

Yes. What's up?

I miss you. She shouldn't have admitted that, but before she could rebuke herself, her phone rang.

It was Billy.

"You're awake? I thought you'd be home and asleep long before now," he said.

"Yeah, me, too."

Her voice must have alerted him to the fact that she was troubled, because he asked, "What's on your mind?"

She regretted disturbing him, especially when she knew how many hours he'd been up dealing with the assorted problems that were all part of owning and operating a restaurant. "You're tired. We can talk about it later."

"Let's talk about it now," he said, encouraging her in that gentle way of his. As exhausted as he was, he sought to comfort her. She couldn't do that. Not after the day he'd had.

"I should never have—"

"Lindy!"

Seeing that she was the one who'd reached out, Billy wasn't going to listen to any excuses. The truth was that she needed a willing ear and so, as briefly as possible, she relayed her conversation with Celeste.

"Sounds to me like your friend is dealing with some major regrets."

"It felt good to tell her I'd forgiven her and Brian, freeing somehow. And I meant it, Billy." She was grateful for the chance to let Celeste know she'd moved on. Forgiveness was one thing, reconciliation was another.

"Do you think the reason she reached out is because she saw you and me on Wednesday?" he asked.

"She mentioned seeing us." Lindy left out the part about finding Billy handsome.

"Did she happen to see the kiss? Bet that blew her mind."

Lindy didn't know what Celeste had seen or not seen. If any mind was blown, it'd been hers. She wasn't mentioning that, either. "It's a possibility. I don't know what she saw; she didn't mention it if she did."

"I thought wanting them to see us was the reason you asked me to kiss you?"

Remembering that kiss made Lindy smile. "As I recall, you weren't overly pleased that I'd blatantly used you."

"True, but that kiss. I have to tell you, Lindy, it shook my world."

"It shook my world, too." A warm sensation washed over her. "Every kiss since then has done the same." Again, she shouldn't be telling Billy this, especially when she'd resolved this was a holiday romance. The fact of the matter was that there was little choice what she would do in the future. She had a signed lease. Her livelihood was in Seattle. And more important, Lindy had a lot to prove to herself and Media Blast. Moving back to Wenatchee after being betrayed by her best friend and Brian, leaving the job she had trained for and emotionally invested in, would feel like she was somehow giving in and admitting defeat. Moving back to Wenatchee would look like she was coming home with her tail between her legs . . . especially when she felt, deep down, that success was around the corner. She couldn't do that. Wouldn't.

"You've grown quiet. What are you thinking?"

"That I should let you get to bed."

"Lindy?"

"Yes?"

"It's late. I'm exhausted and probably shouldn't ask you this." He hesitated, as if even now he was weighing his words.

"Ask me," she said softly.

When he spoke, his voice was so low she had to strain to hear him. "Stay."

"Stay?" she repeated, hoping she'd heard wrong.

"I don't want you to go back to Seattle. I feel like we have the start of something that has real potential. I hate to see it end."

CHAPTER THIRTEEN

The next morning, Lindy slept until ten. Her mother was busy in the kitchen, which made her feel terrible, as she'd intended to help with the meal preparations. Her mother went all out for Christmas and cooked for weeks in advance. Her plates of cookies delivered to friends on Christmas Eve, following the church service, were tradition.

"Mom, you should have woken me." Lindy felt as though she was letting everyone down.

"I heard you talking on the phone last night and it was in the wee hours of the morning. You needed your rest. There's nothing I can't handle on my own. This is supposed to be your vacation, remember?"

Lindy refused to listen; she enjoyed cooking with her mother. Some of her favorite memories with her mom had taken place in this very kitchen. The recipes were ones handed down from her grandparents. From one generation to the next. The special fruit salad, the stuffing that went inside the turkey, and the homemade applesauce were the very dishes Lindy had grown up enjoying. One day she would prepare them for her own family.

"I want to help," Lindy insisted. "Now tell me what you'd like me to do."

Ever organized, her mother had the recipe for the family's favorite corn casserole laid out. Lindy collected what she needed and assembled it, and then placed it in the refrigerator, ready for the oven on Christmas Day.

"Aren't you meeting Peggy for lunch?" her mother said, turning to look at the kitchen clock.

Her mother was right. Lindy needed to get a move on, or she'd be late. Kissing her mother's cheek, Lindy headed out the door, eager to see her friend. Ever since Lindy had arrived, the two had spent a bit of time together each day.

Peggy was already at the pizza parlor when Lindy walked in the door. She'd ordered the margherita pizza they'd agreed on earlier.

"Merry Christmas," Peggy said, smiling up at Lindy.

Pulling out a chair, Lindy took her seat. "Merry Christmas."

The server came to get Lindy's drink order and left. "I

should probably ask for something stronger than diet soda," she said.

"Oh? I got your text from late last night, so tell me what's going on."

Lindy hardly knew where to start. Seeing that it was Christmas Eve, she wasn't willing to weigh down their conversation. Now wasn't the time to think about Celeste. She didn't want to mention her early-morning conversation with Billy, either. Nevertheless, him asking her not to return to Seattle lingered in her mind.

"Stuff. You know. Life in general."

"I'm glad you were able to meet me. Especially today."

"Sure. What's up?"

"I know I casually mentioned this idea before, so I hope you'll indulge me."

This was interesting. "Okay. What idea? Another food scavenger hunt? A game to play at midnight tonight? A pub crawl?"

Peggy smiled and was about to speak when the pizza was delivered. They took a few minutes to enjoy a hot slice before her friend returned her attention to Lindy.

"I have a proposition for you," Peggy said, and seemed to have trouble holding back her excitement. Her face lit up and she all but squirmed in her seat. "And it's one I think you're going to like."

"What kind of proposition?" Lindy couldn't help being

curious, seeing how Peggy's beautiful dark eyes glowed with delight.

Waving her hand, Peggy said, "I don't want you to make a decision right away. You're in town another week, and I want you to promise me you'll use that time to mull this over."

"I'm listening."

"Earlier this week, you helped me with a small glitch on my website that I was having." She mentioned this as if it was something Lindy might have forgotten.

"Yes." It'd taken her all of fifteen minutes to get the information arranged for Peggy the way that worked best. It was nothing. Lindy could have managed it in her sleep.

"Greg, one of the guys in the office, happened to mention it to Marcus, a friend of his who owns the Rose Bud, a flower shop in town." She paused, as if this was of significance. "Greg also told Marcus you'd been the one to work on the Wine Press's website. Now Marcus wants to know if you'd be willing to help him with his website."

Instantly an idea for a flower shop popped into her head like a giant jack-in-the-box, leaping forward. This was exactly the kind of creative work Lindy enjoyed most. The back-end stuff took time and effort, but the graphics portion was the fun part for her, and she was good at it. She wasn't being immodest. Lindy knew her strengths and weaknesses. The CEO at Media Blast saw her work and believed she was the best fit for the company, which was why he'd hired her over Laurie.

"When Greg mentioned it to me, I told him I wouldn't even ask. This is your vacation time, and besides, it's Christmas."

The words went over her head until she realized what Peggy had said. "But you did ask me?" Lindy figured there was a reason her friend had relented.

"And . . . being in the business I'm in, I have contacts with several small-business owners in the area. People who have invested their time, energy, and funds to build opportunity for themselves and their families. These family-operated businesses are the very backbone of America."

Peggy didn't need to sing their praises to Lindy. She could see with her own eyes the hard work and long hours Billy had put into his restaurant. It worried her that he was running himself into the ground, looking to make the most of his investment.

"The problem is that while Marcus is brilliant when it comes to knowing flowers and arranging them in creative, beautiful ways, he knows next to nothing about social media and user-friendly websites. His investment went into starting up his business. Like Billy, he's trying to fit marketing in among running the store, filling orders, and balancing his inventory purchases with cash flow."

"Go on." Lindy had a good idea of what Peggy was about to suggest. She needed, even wanted, her friend to say it, although she wasn't sure what her response would be.

The way the side of Peggy's mouth struggled to hold back a smile, it was as if she could tell Lindy was interested. "Like I mentioned, I wasn't even going to tell you about Marcus and the Rose Bud. You've got a lot going on in your life as it is."

"True . . . but?"

"But then I thought about all the other small businesses in town who badly need services you could provide. Without much effort, I came up with a dozen more opportunities I could easily add to the list, and that's only the start."

"Peggy," Lindy said, holding up her hand to stop her. "I know what you're going to suggest, and I have to admit it's tempting."

"Good—"

"But," Lindy said emphatically, "moving to Wenatchee isn't feasible at this time."

Lindy hated to admit how tempting this all sounded. Regrettably, there were too many factors that made it impossible. On top of the list was the work proposal she'd put together for the Ferguson Group. If that was accepted, it would require weeks, perhaps months, of work.

"All I'm asking is that you think about it."

"Breaking away from a stable income and building a start-up business is a big deal. It takes more than an investment of time. Moving expenses would be involved, and I would leave the company that has put their faith and trust in me. It's no small thing to walk away, Peggy. I know you can understand and appreciate that."

"Of course, I do," Peggy confirmed. "I understand your hesitation and appreciate your loyalty to your employer, especially considering how hard the others on the team have been to work with. You could give them proper notice, ease your way."

"Owning my own business is a huge financial risk."

"It is." Again, Peggy agreed. "Not everyone has the ambition and the drive to make it a huge success, but I think you do. Furthermore, you'd be helping others succeed. That has got its own share of rewards."

Lindy believed that, too, but that didn't resolve other pressing questions she would need to answer first.

"There's my apartment," Lindy said, thinking out loud. As appealing as this was, all she could see were the obstacles standing in her way. "I signed a year's lease for my apartment and I'm only halfway through it."

"Didn't you mention that apartments are at a premium in Seattle and how fortunate you were to find one within your price range?"

"Yes, it was the great apartment search."

"You wouldn't have a problem subleasing it, if necessary, would you?"

Lindy hadn't considered that. Shortly after she'd moved in, two of her coworkers had asked if there were other apartments available in the same complex. Without a doubt, either one of them would be happy to take over her lease.

"It's more than subleasing my apartment," Lindy said, not looking at Peggy, for fear her friend would read the eagerness in her eyes. Peggy did make a move sound possible.

"I know," Peggy responded, with an understanding that caused Lindy to glance upward.

"You do?" she asked.

"It's about Celeste and Brian."

Lindy waved off that excuse. "I've forgiven them. It's in the past and nothing I want to discuss. It's over."

"Maybe so, but deep down I think you're afraid if you move back home, they'll assume it's because of them. That you've been unable to put the past behind you. It would be like admitting you hadn't been able to deal with what they did, even though you have."

"Like saying they won and I lost," Lindy said, and realized there might be some truth in that. How intuitive Peggy was. While she didn't want to believe it, there was a possibility Peggy was right.

Her friend appreciated what she was saying. Making this change would require a lot of soul-searching on Lindy's part. Her head was full of Christmas, and if she'd admit it, her budding relationship with Billy, too. Once the holidays were over and she was back in Seattle, that would be the time to weigh this decision. She couldn't, wouldn't, before then.

"You have time," Peggy said, once again interrupting Lindy's meandering thoughts. "I'm bringing it up now so you'll consider the possibilities."

Lindy nodded. "I will, I promise." And she would give it serious thought, especially if the Ferguson Group went with their competitors. More than one company had put in a bid for this major account, and getting it would be a coup for Media Blast and for her future with the company.

"I have a couple more little incentives for you to think about while you're at it."

"Incentives? Such as?"

"Do you remember when we first met?"

That was a silly question if ever there was one. "Of course. Grade school."

"I mean the very first day."

Searching her memory, Lindy came up blank and shook her head.

"My family had moved to Wenatchee from Tennessee, and we were one of only a handful of Black families in the neighborhood. My first day of school, I didn't see a single other person who looked like me. I felt like the odd girl out. I'd never felt more alone or out of place.

"At lunch, I sat at a table by myself. Then you slid your tray down next to me and asked if I had a pair of Roller-blades. When I said I did, you invited me to come to your house. You were my very first real friend here."

"I did?" Lindy didn't remember that, but then it'd been years ago. Lindy had loved hearing Peggy's southern accent, which over the years had completely disappeared. "All I remember is what fun we had and how quickly you became my best friend."

"And mine," Peggy echoed. "Now it's time for me to repay the favor."

Lindy wasn't sure she understood. The question must have shown on her expression, because Peggy went on to explain.

"It's my turn to be your friend when you need one. I see how much you've opened up and become freer since you've been here. I hate to see you go back and get sucked into the machine that stole your joy."

Lindy knew that was true. She'd asked Santa for a best friend, and then right after she'd written it down, she'd run into Peggy. Immediately it was like old times. It felt as if they'd never been apart. The evenings she'd spent with Peggy's other friends, Chloe and Jayne, had been just the tonic she'd needed. Chloe and Jayne had welcomed her as if Lindy had always been a part of their small group.

"Even if I did move back to town . . ." Lindy said, thinking out loud. While it was understood she could live with her parents for as long as needed, doing that didn't feel right. It would be a giant step backward, living in her childhood home.

"Even if what?" Peggy pried, unwilling to allow Lindy to drop the thought.

"Where would I live? Yes, I could move back in with my parents, but that's the last thing I want. Don't get me wrong, I love my family. They're great, but I'm closer to thirty than twenty-five. The last thing I expected when I graduated from college was needing to move home."

"That's the best part of my plan."

"Oh, how's that?"

"I was saving this until last," Peggy announced. "I need a roommate."

Lindy had been to Peggy's spacious apartment, which was nearly double the size of hers in Seattle. Additionally, it had two bedrooms and was in an excellent neighborhood, above a retail section in the renovated part of town. The restaurant, grocery, and shopping center below made it possible to collect essentials without having to drive. An ideal location and situation. Because the complex was new, Lindy wasn't sure she could even afford half the rent.

"What's your rent?" she asked.

Peggy told her, and it was half of what Lindy paid in Seattle. If she were to share it, that meant it would be half again as much. A quarter of what she paid for housing in the Seattle area.

"That's reasonable," she was forced to admit. "But there's no guarantee I'd get enough work to support myself for a few months. I have savings but—"

Peggy stopped her. "Trust me, between Greg and me, we can get you enough work for the next six months, and that's without trying. This area is clamoring for someone to help with social media and website management. You'd be filling a real need."

Peggy appeared to have it all figured out. Lindy appreciated that Peggy was giving her the space and time to consider this idea.

"You notice I didn't mention the real kicker. The one point I think will probably be the strongest incentive for you leaving Seattle." Peggy gave her a knowing look.

"And exactly what would that be?"

Peggy's smile took up her entire face. "Billy Kincade. He's crazy about you, and if I can read the signs, which I have been known to do on occasion, you feel the same about him."

Lindy was admitting nothing. "We've had a few good times," she said, with some reluctance. Peggy had read her like a cartoon caption. Billy asking her to stay was definitely on the table, although Lindy didn't want to admit it out loud.

"Then I say let the good times roll with Billy and with me . . . I'll wait until you make your decision before I look for a roommate."

That was fair. Lindy agreed with a quick nod. "You've certainly given me something to think about."

"Good. Now go have a wonderful Christmas with your family and we'll connect in a couple days."

Lindy nodded. "And, Peggy, thank you for your friendship and support—you don't know how much it means to me."

By then their pizza was cold and Lindy gave the packaged leftovers to Peggy. They left the pizza parlor together. Peggy headed out to her parents' house. Lindy started toward where she'd parked her car.

As she crossed the street, her gaze fell upon Santa. He had parked next to her. She'd seen him enter the pizza parlor. It was the same Santa she'd met while in Leavenworth. She'd recognized him right away.

"Merry Christmas, Santa," she said, coming to stand alongside him.

Turning to look her way, he smiled and gave a cheery "Ho, ho, ho." Santa retrieved a large bag from the truck bed and swung it over his shoulder and waited for her.

"Oh yes, I remember you," he said, smiling at her.

"I saw you on Wednesday in Leavenworth."

"Yes, yes. You mentioned that you'd written me a letter."

"But you hadn't read it yet."

"Ah, but I have now, and seeing that you've been a good girl all year, I'm happy to grant your every wish."

"Thanks, Santa." This was fun. This guy definitely played his part well.

"I recall an earlier letter from your childhood when you asked for Rollerblades." He rubbed his hand down the side of his beard, as if checking his memory.

Rollerblades were likely the most popular request Santa had received during her childhood years. "You should know I broke my arm while learning to operate those skates," she said, enjoying teasing him.

"That's not the only thing that's been broken, now, is it?"

"The only bone," she said, not getting what he referenced.

"Ah, but one's tattered heart can hurt as badly as a broken bone."

Lindy blinked and studied him more closely. "You seem to know a lot about me, Santa."

In response he grinned. "Say, young lady, how are you at handing out candy canes to little boys and girls?"

"Why do you ask?"

"Well, for one thing, I'm in need of an assistant, and for another, I believe you've got something weighing on your mind. Perhaps what you need is a listening ear."

Santa was right. Perhaps she did.

CHAPTER FOURTEEN

The long line of adults with small children awaited Santa's arrival at the Children's Closet clothing store, where he was set to make his appearance. He handed Lindy a Santa hat and a bucket of candy canes. Her job was to manage the line, making sure each child had time with him.

When Santa had first asked for her help, Lindy had hesitated. Yet, there was something about the way he'd studied her, as if he knew the decision that weighed on her mind. He just might have a word of wisdom to share, and she certainly was willing to listen.

Once Santa was in place and the children took their turns, one by one, Lindy found herself caught up in the magic of the moment. It surprised her how much she enjoyed the exchanges Santa had with the children and their parents. He played his part perfectly. She'd never seen any-one do it better. He asked the children questions and seemed to recognize several as he asked things only an in-sider would know. She remembered her own time with him while in Leavenworth and how he seemed to know her. He was good, she'd say that. Really good with chil-dren and adults alike.

Most of the kids were eager to visit Santa, while others clung to their mothers, terrified of the man in the red suit with the long white beard.

"Do you have a special Christmas wish for Santa?" she asked the next child in line, who waited patiently. The lit-tle girl, who looked to be about five, nodded enthusiasti-cally. "It's a secret; I can only tell Santa."

"He's a good listener," Lindy assured her.

"I wrote him a letter, too."

"So did I," Lindy told her.

"Did he read it?" she asked, her eyes round and curi-ous.

"He did," Lindy said with a smile.

When it was her turn, she raced up to Santa and leaped onto his lap. Lindy couldn't hear what the child said, but Santa got a big belly laugh out of it and gave her a gentle hug before he sent her on her way.

One little boy stuck out in Lindy's mind. He seemed sad and preoccupied.

"My sister is sick," the little boy said. "If you can help her get well, then I don't need anything for Christmas."

Santa nodded, as if he was well aware of the sick little girl. "I'm sorry little Anna needs surgery, but you know what?" he said, "I believe she is going to get the very best care possible and that she'll be home soon. Don't you worry."

"Thank you, Santa."

"And, Buddy, I think you need to check under the Christmas tree later. Santa hasn't forgotten you."

Hearing the conversation, at first Lindy was alarmed that he might be giving the child false hope, but then she saw how the little boy brightened with the news. At least he would have hope for Christmas. Silently, Lindy sent up a prayer, asking God to heed Santa's words.

There wasn't any need for a photographer, as all the parents had phones, snapping dozens of pictures in the few minutes their children spent on Santa's lap. The lack of a photographer made Lindy wonder how Santa was being paid for his time and energy, and then realized the store probably compensated him.

Santa's patience with the children amazed her. Even the crying, squirming ones. He comforted each fussy child in a way that soon had them staring up at him with faces filled with wide-eyed wonder.

Santa was booked for three hours, and the time flew. It

felt like Lindy had been assisting him for minutes when the shop owner announced the time was up. The store was closing early for Christmas Eve.

"We can't thank you enough, Santa," the woman said. "You don't know what this means to us and our small shop."

"I enjoyed every minute," Santa returned.

"Are you sure you won't take anything . . . We did a number of big sales while you were here."

He held up his hand, stopping her. "It's my pleasure."

So Santa wasn't being compensated. He'd volunteered his time. That he would do this for the children on his own deeply impressed Lindy.

She handed Santa the bucket with only a few remaining candy canes. "You were wonderful," she said, in appreciation of his patience and charm with each one of the children.

"Been at this awhile," Santa said, as he stood and stretched, working his shoulders back and forth.

"It shows."

"Now, my dear, it's your turn."

"Are you sure? You must be exhausted."

He checked the time. "Not at all. I loved seeing the children, but I'll need to watch the clock. I've got a busy night ahead of me."

Santa must have a long list of appearances lined up.

"Let's grab a cup of hot chocolate and chat for a bit."
He led the way, even before she could refuse.

The small coffee shop across the street was open, and
he held the door for Lindy. She should have realized Santa
would be nothing less than a gentleman.

"Allow me," Lindy said, as she started toward the
counter to place their order.

"Nonsense, I owe you for your help this afternoon," he
insisted. "Besides, Santa rarely gets charged. People seem
to think one good deed will wipe out all their transgres-
sions for the year." He chuckled and escorted her to a
table, pulling out the chair for her to take a seat.

As he approached the counter to order their drinks,
Lindy mulled over what she could possibly tell him, or if
she should say anything. And like Santa, she needed to
watch the time. Billy had asked her to stop by the Wine
Press that afternoon, plus she needed to get home early
enough to help her mother set up for the church group following the evening candlelight service.

Santa returned with two mugs of steaming cocoa and
set them down on the table. Once he was seated, his gaze
settled firmly on her. His look was gentle, understanding,
sympathetic. "Now tell me what's got you all twisted up
inside. Decisions don't need to be difficult, you realize,
once you weigh the pros and cons."

If it were only that easy. "What makes you think I have

a decision to make?" she asked, tilting her head to one side as she studied him. This man seemed to know far more about her than he should.

"I'm Santa," he said, as if that was all the explanation necessary.

Lindy wasn't that easily bamboozled. She had to assume he'd overheard her and Peggy's conversation at the pizza parlor.

"You have a choice to make. Do you like living in the big city?"

"I like Seattle."

He nodded, encouraging her to continue. "I enjoy the cultural advantages available there. Celeste and I . . ." She'd been about to mention the Broadway shows they'd been able to attend, the sporting events, the shopping, and the fine restaurants. They splurged once a month on a fun outing. Lindy badly missed those girlfriend times. Going out with guys was a completely different experience than with her best friend.

"Ah, Celeste," he said, and shook his head. "She proved to be a real disappointment, didn't she?"

She nodded, preferring not to get into the past. Santa had definitely been listening in on her conversation with Peggy. Although she didn't remember mentioning her former roommate.

"What about Media Blast? Is that what's holding you back?"

She had to wonder how Santa figured out she worked for Media Blast. Seeing how much of her conversation he'd listened in on—she was tempted to ask if he enjoyed his pizza with or without anchovies.

"Lindy?" Santa asked.

She realized he was waiting for her reply.

"Not entirely. They pay well, and I enjoy my work." This was getting a bit eerie, that Santa would know all this. She returned his stare, which he held with gentle patience. Lindy was the first one to blink.

"Starting your own business would require a giant leap of faith. It would be a huge risk. The thing is, Lindy, you're fully capable of making it a success if you do decide to go for it."

His confidence nearly drew tears to her eyes.

"But," he said, "isn't there something more—rather, someone—who makes this decision even more difficult? You want to give this new romance a chance and hesitate at the risk you'll be taking. Am I right?"

Lindy lowered her gaze to her drink, preferring not to answer.

"Billy Kincade isn't the same rascal he was at ten. He's reformed his ways and learned some hard life lessons along the way. I have to say I'm rather proud of that young man."

Oh yes, Billy. He'd been with her in Leavenworth when she'd first seen Santa. She'd already decided not to mention Peggy's idea to Billy, knowing he'd already asked her to stay. He wanted her to leave Seattle and move back to Wenatchee. The temptation was to give in, leave all that she'd worked toward in Seattle behind, and basically start over from the ground up.

"It's more than this young man, though, right?"

Good grief, Santa must have been sitting right next to her to have this much information.

"There's a large project I submitted a proposal for that has yet to be accepted," she said. A huge investment of her time, effort, and skill had gone into this bid. She'd waited a long time for the chance to work on a project like this. Now it felt as if she were standing on a cliff: afraid to look down, afraid to move, afraid to breathe, not knowing which way to turn.

"It appears you have a lot to think about, Lindy."

"I do," she agreed, seeing that he was finished with his drink and looked ready to go. "I appreciate you listening."

"I was happy to be a sounding board."

"You're very good, Santa."

He shrugged off her praise and scooted back his chair.

Lindy stood, too, leaving her mug half-full of cocoa. They left the coffee shop together and walked toward the street-level parking complex.

It was already late; the sky was darkening. By four-thirty it would be pitch-dark. Lindy had always loved winters in the Pacific Northwest for the opportunity to view the northern lights. She didn't get a chance to see them in Seattle because the city lights made it impossible.

"Thanks again, Santa," she said, as he approached his truck. "Have a good night."

"Always. Best night of the year for me and the missus. Plan for it starting every January. And, listen, if you do decide to take that big leap of faith, you write me a letter and let me know. I've always enjoyed your letters."

Lindy waited for the interior of her car to warm up and the windows to defrost before she headed to see Billy.

He'd told her the restaurant was booked with reservations, so she wasn't surprised that it took her a few minutes to find a parking spot. What did come as a shock was how busy the bar area seemed to be on Christmas Eve. One would think most people would want to be home with family. Billy was pouring wine, and when he noticed her, his face eased into a welcoming smile. They'd both gone into this with the thought it would be nothing more than a holiday romance. Somewhere, somehow, in the last few days that had changed. For Billy, and as reluctant as she was to admit it, for Lindy, too.

Not wanting to distract him, she slipped onto a bar stool and waited until he'd filled an order before he approached her.

"Hey," he said, his eyes lighting up as they settled on her.

"Merry Christmas," she returned.

"Merry Christmas," he said. A couple minutes later, his replacement appeared, and he came around the bar to join her.

Taking her by the hand, Billy led her into his office and closed the door. Right away she was in his arms. He kissed her as if this were the final scene of a romantic Christmas movie. Her arms went around his neck as she surrendered herself to his lips, giving as well as taking.

"Wow," she breathed, when they eventually broke apart. "What was that for?"

"Missed you," he whispered.

It'd been less then twenty-four hours since they'd last been together. It made her wonder how he'd react when it was days or even weeks before they could see each other again. In her heart of hearts, she recognized that long-distance romances rarely survived beyond a few weeks or months.

"You're busy."

"It won't be so hectic next week," he promised. "I'll take time off so we can be together. Didn't I hear you promise Peter a sledding adventure? I volunteer to tag along."

Lindy doubted Billy knew what he was getting himself into. "You're on."

"I've always loved the snow and was into snowboarding for a while."

So much of his life, his likes and dislikes, were un-known to her. She hoped to learn more and share more of herself. Billy seemed to want to make the most of the va-cation time she had left, and Lindy did as well. What the week following Christmas, before she returned to Seattle, would mean for their future, Lindy couldn't tell. Of one thing she was certain: Spending that extra time with Billy would make her decision all the more difficult.

"I'll be by your parents' house tomorrow to play Santa for Peter," he said, reminding her that he'd volunteered to give her nephew the thrill he would long remember.

"Chad and Ashley plan to arrive around noon, so you could come any time after that." She seemed to remem-ber her mother suggesting he arrive around three and she selfishly didn't want to wait until midafternoon to see him.

"I'll be there with bells on," he said, smiling down on her.

"Funny you should mention Santa," she said. "I ran into him today."

"Oh? Just remember the only Santa for you is me."

She must have had a funny look because he grew seri-ous.

"Don't tell me you fell for this other Santa?"

"No, silly. It was the same Santa from Leavenworth. He seemed to know about the letters I wrote him . . . I'm being ridiculous." She shook her head to clear her thoughts. "Santa needed my help with one of his appearances. He was amazing with all the children."

"That's what makes Santa Santa," Billy said. "Every kid writes Santa at one time or another, so the fact that he mentioned your letters is all part of his routine."

"You're right." Still, Lindy wasn't fully convinced. It was far more than that, more than she wanted to explain. Santa had seemed to know more about her than what was feasible. Most likely, there was a logical explanation. He must have eaten at the pizza parlor, although she didn't remember seeing him seated. Dressed as he was, he would be hard to miss.

"Shall we head for the city park on the twenty-sixth?" Billy asked, taking her mind off Santa and back to the promise she'd made to Peter.

"Sure." Lindy didn't have any other plans, and Peter had asked her several times already when they would be going. "That sounds great. Are you sure you can get away?"

"I'll make it work," he said.

Lindy knew Billy had been putting in a lot of extra hours because of the holidays. He needed the break. "If it doesn't work that you can get the time off, I'll understand. What's important is you and the Wine Press." She meant that from her heart. "We have all next week," she reminded him.

"Seven days doesn't seem near long enough," he said.

"I'm already dreading the thought of you returning to Seattle."

No matter what her decision was, Lindy realized, she would need to go back.

Billy closed his eyes as if the news was unwelcome. "I guess it's wrong of me to want you to stay."

"Not wrong, Billy. It makes me happy you feel that way. It's just that Seattle is where I live."

He lowered his head. "I don't know how often I'll be able to get away, especially on a weekend."

"I know." She was well aware of the limitation with him owning and operating the Wine Press. He needed to be available to his staff and customers on the two busiest days and nights of the week. His day off was Wednesday, and it was highly unlikely he would be able to drive to Seattle and back on the same day.

Lindy knew it would be a mistake to mention Peggy's idea. If she chose to not start her own small business, he might consider this her way of saying she wasn't interested in them as a couple. That couldn't be further from the truth.

Lindy left the restaurant and then drove home, her thoughts heavy. She shook them off, determined to make the most of Christmas Eve. How could she not, seeing she was with her family for the biggest celebration of the year: the birth of baby Jesus.

CHAPTER FIFTEEN

Her mother served a light dinner of sliced meats and cheeses so they would be ready for the Christmas Eve church service. Traditionally, her parents invited their Sunday school class over, following the church service, for cookies and hot cider. Her mother had been baking cookies for weeks, storing them in the freezer so she could send a plate heaping with an assortment of cookies home with each guest.

Chad, Ashley, and Peter were set to meet them at the church before heading over to Ashley's parents' house for her family's celebration. Ashley had four siblings, and it was sure to be chaotic and fun.

Even before entering the church building, Lindy could hear the choir singing. The steepled church was brightly lit, both inside and out. The manger scene was arranged in the snow outside the building, and a light dusting started to fall in lazy, wind-tossed flakes, floating down from the heavens.

Glancing up, she marveled at how perfect the night was. The burden of the future seemed far removed. She knew that whatever her decision, it didn't need to be made that night, or tomorrow. As she looked toward the babe in the manager, she knew He would guide her.

Christmas Eve was a time of joy and celebration. A time for family. A time to count her blessings, of which there were many. It hadn't been an easy year, and she was just as glad to put it behind her, and yet there was much for which to be grateful. It had just taken her awhile to see and appreciate it.

The service started with the singing of long-familiar Christmas carols. "O Holy Night," "Away in a Manger," and "We Three Kings" were some of Lindy's favorites. She noticed some of the children were already dressed in their pajamas and slippers. She remembered coming to the evening service in her own nightclothes, in what seemed another lifetime ago.

After the Christmas Eve service, she and Chad would be eager for bed, knowing that if they went to sleep right away, the morning would come quicker, and they would be able to open their presents from Santa. Chad had still been young enough to believe in Santa, and for his sake, Lindy pretended to believe, too. She wanted her little brother to have the same wonderful Christmas experiences she'd had.

The church service was everything she knew it would be. As she walked out of the church, her gaze once again went to the life-sized Nativity scene on the snow-covered lawn. There, kneeling next to the manger, was the man she readily recognized as the Santa she'd met earlier that day. She turned to tell her mother, but when she looked back, he was gone.

"Lindy, did you need something?" her mother asked.

She shook her head. "I thought I saw someone I knew. Guess not."

From the church, several families headed to the Carmichaels' house. It wasn't long before every spot in both the living and family rooms were taken. Lindy helped serve, enjoying the myriad conversations as she went about the room, refilling cups and passing around a plate of cookies.

"It's so good to see you, Lindy." She heard that again and again, and it never grew old. Most of these friends of her parents were ones Lindy had known nearly her entire life. They were as close to family as one could get without a blood connection.

It was after eleven before the house was quiet once

again. Lindy sent her parents to bed, as they were overly tired from the day's activities. She cleared the plates and cups, filled the dishwasher and set it to wash, then headed toward her bedroom, too. Sitting up in bed, she looked over at her nightstand and saw the letter she'd written to Santa just a week earlier.

She reached for it and started to read again.

Dear Santa . . .

Unlike her childhood, Lindy slept in late on Christmas morning. With sheer determination, she managed to focus on the holiday and put any decision-making off for another time. Today was for family and fun.

Her mother already had the turkey roasting when Lindy made her way into the kitchen.

"Merry Christmas, Mom," she said, and gave her mother a peck on the cheek.

"Merry Christmas," her mother echoed. "I believe this is the best Christmas ever."

Her mother said the same thing every year.

"I believe it is, too," Lindy said, and this Christmas she felt it more so than any other. Her life had seemed to have made a positive turn. No matter what happened with Media Blast, she knew she'd given this latest project her best shot. Knowing that was what mattered most.

"Dad's making breakfast."

He sat in his recliner, next to the flickering fire in the brick fireplace, his iPad in his hand. "Just waiting for Sleeping Beauty to make an appearance," he said.

Her dad's sourdough hotcakes were not to be missed. Her mother started sizzling the bacon. Within fifteen minutes they'd gathered around the kitchen table, passing butter and pure, warmed maple syrup.

They'd decided to wait for Chad, Ashley, and Peter before opening the gifts. Seeing that the family would arrive at about noon, Lindy helped her mother get all the side dishes ready and the table set. She added an extra place setting on the off chance Billy could join them.

Right on the dot, Chad, Ashley, and Peter arrived. Sleepy from the drive, Peter waddled over, yawning loudly, to hug Lindy.

"Did Santa arrive at your house this morning?" she asked, picking him up and balancing him against her hip.

He nodded with another big yawn. "I got a fire truck and LEGOs and new pajamas."

"Anything on your list that Santa forgot?" she asked. Knowing he loved working the wooden puzzles, she'd gotten him four that were currently under the tree. Her parents had wrapped up a child-style teepee tent for him that would fit nicely in his playroom. Peter would love that. He'd seen one in a catalog and had run to show his grandma.

He was late for his nap, so Lindy settled them both in the rocking chair. Peter closed his eyes and started to drift off to sleep, all the while protesting. He wanted to open his presents, pointing toward the Christmas tree.

"I want more presents," he said with a pout.

"Take your nap first, and then we'll open all the gifts. Okay?"

Asking was a mistake. "No, I want to open them now."

"Sh-h-h, in a little bit," she whispered, and continued to rock. It wasn't long before he stopped fussing and fell into a deep sleep. Content, Lindy brushed the soft hair from his forehead and continued to gently hold him against her heart.

Soon after Peter was asleep, her brother approached her. "Let me take him. I'll put him down in my old room."

"Don't you dare," Lindy mouthed back. Holding the sleeping toddler in her arms was both comfortable and relaxing. Sitting by the warm fire, with Peter nestled in her arms, Lindy soon felt sleepy herself. Beau snuggled at the base of the chair. This was about as close to tranquility as she could imagine.

After an hour her nephew woke, sat up, and rubbed his eyes. "Can we open the gifts now?" he asked, eager to get off Lindy's lap. "You said we could after I woke up."

"I'm going to need an assistant to help distribute all

these presents," her father said, walking over to the gaily decorated tree. He picked up one of the wrapped gifts and looked to Peter.

"I can do it," Peter said, eager to be helpful.

"Thank you, Peter," her dad said. "I'll read off the names and you can deliver them. Sound good?"

Peter nodded, nearly bouncing on his feet with anticipation.

As his grandfather read off the names, Peter stumbled back and forth from the evergreen Christmas tree to deliver each gift. Then, taking turns, one at a time, they opened the presents with Beau's help.

Lindy waited patiently for her family to unwrap the gifts she'd purchased.

Her parents were thrilled with the bottle of wine and the gift certificate for dinner at the Wine Press.

"We've been wanting to have dinner there ever since it opened."

"I heard it's almost impossible to get a reservation," Chad commented, reading over the certificate.

"It helps if you're dating the owner," Lindy told them. Billy had insisted on compensating her for the work she'd done on his web page, and she was happy to accept, knowing how pleased this gift certificate would make her parents.

After they'd opened all their gifts, Ashley and Lindy

helped in the kitchen. Lindy was busy peeling the potatoes when her phone beeped.

Let me know when you're ready for Santa to arrive.

Anytime. I'll meet you outside first. Text when you're here.

Okay.

Lindy had set aside one of the puzzles for Santa to give Peter and a small gift for the unborn baby, too. She planned to meet Billy and give him the gifts before he came into the house.

About thirty minutes later, Billy's text arrived.

Lindy silently slipped outside with the small bundle of presents. She didn't take the time to put on her coat and wrapped her sweater tightly around her as she met Billy in the driveway, dressed in his Santa suit, complete with the long white beard and an abundance of white hair.

"Hey there, handsome," she said, her heart lifting with happiness. She thought this Christmas couldn't get any better, and now it did the minute she saw Billy.

"You like the beard?" he asked, lowering it a fraction so he could lean forward and kiss her. He placed his arms around her to protect her from the wind and cold.

"I can live without all that hair on your face," she teased.

"Matter of fact, so can I."

"Can you stay for dinner?" She didn't want to take him away from his own family but was selfish enough to long to spend time with him this Christmas.

He nodded. "Already saw Dede and the kids, so I'm all yours."

All yours. Although that was a figure of speech, Lindy held the words to her heart, recognizing how strongly attached she was to Billy in such a short amount of time. After a week, it felt as if he'd always been in her life, and perhaps he had been, in the back of her mind.

"I'm wearing the Santa costume over my clothes, so once Santa visits Peter, I'll leave and then return as myself."

"That's perfect." She was grateful he'd thought this through before he arrived.

Sneaking back into the house, Lindy was happy to see that Peter was sitting on the floor, playing with his Matchbox cars on the zigzag racetrack, a gift from Lindy's mom and dad. She mouthed the words "Santa's here" to her parents, who smiled and nodded.

Not five minutes after her return, the doorbell rang. Her dad shared a look with Lindy, and she winked back. "I can't imagine who that would be," he said.

Beau barked and raced to the front of the house, eager to greet the company.

"Who do you think would visit on Christmas Day?" her mother asked Peter.

The little boy shrugged but looked up at his grandfather with questioning eyes.

"Do you want to answer the door with me?"

Peter nodded, and awkwardly rose to his feet before racing to the front door with his grandfather.

Lindy heard Peter gasp before he stormed back into the family room and shouted, "It's Santa! It's Santa!"

"Ho! Ho! Ho!" Santa called out enthusiastically, as he came into the house. "I understand there's a good little boy named Peter who's visiting his grandma and grandpa."

Peter stared up at Santa, his eyes as wide as he could stretch them, his mouth open in awe and wonder.

"Santa has gifts for good little girls and boys." He lifted the bag off his shoulder and, reaching inside, pulled out the gift Lindy had given him for Peter. The four-year-old fell to his knees and tore apart the paper.

"And here's another," Santa said, handing an envelope to Chad and Ashley along with a receiving blanket for the baby yet to be born.

Ashley opened it and shared it with Chad. "A gift certificate for dinner at the Wine Press . . . wow."

"Thanks, Santa."

"And here's another one," he said, handing a bottle of wine to her father and mother.

"You're kidding," her dad said, as he read the label. "We're saving this for a special occasion." He showed it to Lindy. "Here's one last gift," he said, extracting a small, wrapped box that he handed to Lindy.

"For me?" she said, unable to hide her surprise.

Billy's eyes held hers. "Yes, you."

Lindy sat with the gift in her lap and carefully unwrapped it. She found a charm bracelet with a single charm. A tiny silver Santa.

"Thought you could add another charm every Christmas," Santa explained.

For Christmas, this year, after reading those long-ago letters, the Santa charm was perfect. "Thank you," she said softly, and then, forgetting herself, she leaned over and kissed him.

"Mommy, Mommy, Aunt Lindy kissed Santa."

"Lucky Santa," Billy murmured, as he headed toward the door.

"Thank you, Santa." Peter hurried forward and grabbed hold of Santa's leg.

Chad gently pried him away so Santa could make his departure.

Santa laughed and left with another cheerful "Ho, ho, ho."

When Billy returned, Peter raced to his side. "Billy, you just missed seeing Santa. He came to the house."

Billy did a good job of looking surprised. "I missed seeing Santa?"

Peter nodded. "Maybe he'll come back."

"That would be a real surprise," Billy said, and winked at Lindy.

———

Dinner was over, the dishes washed, and everyone lounged around with full bellies, needing a break before digging into a selection of desserts. Her mother had baked several pies, plus there were cookies and a variety of Christmas candies.

Billy and Lindy sat on the sofa, his arm around her shoulders. She wore the charm bracelet. She had gotten him a small gift: a certificate to update his website the next time she was in town.

A Christmas movie played on the television. Peter was sprawled across his mother's and father's laps, half asleep. Her mother had her fingers working on her latest knitting project, and her dad was involved in the hardcover novel by his favorite author. Lindy knew he wouldn't be able to resist checking out the book.

"You know what we need to do," Chad said, extracting himself from Peter and his wife. "Scrabble."

"Scrabble?" Billy repeated.

"It's tradition," Lindy explained. "Every Christmas we all play Scrabble."

"And work on a jigsaw puzzle," her dad added.

The puzzle was set up on a card table close to the fireplace. This year, the picture was of Santa coming down the chimney into a living room fully decorated for the holidays. Before dinner, her dad had gotten it going and had started working on the border. Chad had added the entire Christmas tree section near the left-hand side of the border.

Billy had added a few pieces himself. Rarely was the puzzle completely assembled by the end of Christmas Day. It took the week between the two holidays to set the thousand pieces in place and complete the picture. Tradition. The puzzle and a rousing game of Scrabble.

Chad set up the Scrabble board on the dining room table and spread out all the small wooden letters.

"You going to join us, Billy?" Chad asked.

Billy looked to Lindy. "What are the stakes?"

"We play for the privilege of hoping we can beat Dad," Lindy explained. "This is his game, and he's practically unstoppable."

"Watch out for Lindy, too. She can be a creative speller."

"Very funny, little brother," she teased back.

Soon the lethargy had left and the six sat around the table while Peter watched cartoons. He bounced between his toys and the television as the game started.

Lindy pulled the *Q* without a *U*, and her first word on the board gained her a whopping six points. Not a great start. Her dad's first word gained him thirteen points. And so it went for the next hour as the board continued to grow with words built up around other words. Once or twice Lindy tried to pull a fast one, insisting her word was in the Webster's dictionary and was quickly proven wrong. It came as no surprise that her father claimed the crown as the top Scrabble player.

"Has he ever lost?" Billy asked Lindy.

"Once. To Mom, and I think he let her win."

"He most certainly did not!" her mother insisted, with a quiver to her lips that said everything.

"Chad was born nine months later," Lindy whispered to Billy.

"Your timing is off by a few years, Lindy." It seemed her mother had overheard.

"Anyone ready for dessert?"

Billy placed his hands on his flat stomach. "Not long ago I swore I couldn't swallow another bite."

"And now?"

"I got a look at that caramel-pecan pie sitting on the kitchen counter and I've decided to make the effort."

"Big of you," Lindy teased.

"I'll take pumpkin," Chad said. "Never did appreciate the fancy pies. Give me apple or pumpkin and I'm a happy man."

The table was cleared, and the desserts were brought out. Lindy went for the caramel-pecan pie. It tasted as good as the recipe promised.

Soon afterward, Chad and his family headed home. Peter was worn out from all the activity and the excitement of the day. Lindy could tell Ashley was tired, too, as her hand continued to rub the slight swell of her pregnancy belly.

After her brother left, Lindy and Billy cuddled together in front of the television. At ten, her parents excused themselves and went to bed.

"Do you think they left for our benefit?" Billy asked, as he kissed the side of her neck.

"Could be." That was likely not the case. Her mother had put in a long day and hadn't napped when most everyone else had taken a short snooze.

"I'll thank them later," Billy murmured, close to her ear.

"Pray tell, what do you have in mind, Billy Kincade?"

"If you could read my thoughts, I'd definitely be getting a bag of coal from Santa next Christmas."

Lindy couldn't hold back a smile had she tried. "Is that so?"

"You have no idea."

"Actually, I think I just might."

Turning her into his arms, Billy kissed her again and again. A commercial played on the television, louder than expected, which broke them apart.

"I have to say, this is the best Christmas I can remember in a long while."

"Mine, too," she said.

"It's because of you, Lindy. I'm doing my best to ignore the fact that you're returning to Seattle in a week."

"Me, too," she admitted.

He reached for her wrist where he'd placed the charm bracelet with the single Santa charm. "My hope is that I'll be the one adding charms every Christmas until it weighs down your arm to the point you can no longer lift it."

Lindy didn't know what to say. Basically, Billy was telling her he wanted to be part of her life from this point forward.

"We've been together a week, Billy," she reminded him. "You can't say something like that after such a short time."

His eyes were dark and serious. "What you don't understand, Lindy, is that you wrote your name on my heart when I was nine years old."

CHAPTER SIXTEEN

The day after Christmas, Lindy had promised to take Peter to the park for fun in the snow. This time of year, there was rarely a lack of the white powder in Wenatchee.

Knowing Peggy was anxious to hear from her, she sent her friend a text.

Out with Peter and Billy. Promise to connect soon. And yes, I am considering what we talked about. Still unsure what's best.

A decision this big couldn't be made on impulse or on the spur of the moment. Lindy needed time to consider her options. In addition, she felt it was necessary to hear the feedback on the project she'd submitted through Media Blast before she could make a decision either way. Yes, it was tempting to give in, but she needed to analyze the ramifications. Peggy was right, Billy would play a part in her decision. Living closer to family, too, of course. Nevertheless, the lure of success, of seeing her work on websites for major businesses, tugged at her. This had been her dream. Her goal from college, and she didn't know if she was ready to give all that up.

Although Peggy had mentioned she would wait on Lindy's decision before finding a roommate, Lindy realized she wouldn't be able to put Peggy off for long. One thing was sure, she couldn't give her friend a definitive answer this week, or probably next week, either.

An entire day spent with Billy and Peter filled her with eager anticipation. How quickly her thoughts had become entangled with him. It was as if they were meant to be together. It felt as if she belonged with Billy.

"Morning, sunshine," she said when he picked up. It was barely eight, and she wasn't sure if he was even awake yet. He hadn't left her parents' house until well after midnight. He'd had a long week, with late hours, and she hated to wake him.

"Morning," he grumbled back. He yawned into the phone, which told her either he'd just woken or he'd recently gotten out of bed.

"Was thinking we should get an early start."

"Good idea. The hills in the park are sure to be busy."

Especially in the week between the holidays with a

cover of fresh snow. As a teenager, Lindy and her friends spent nearly every day of their winter vacation from school in the snow. Lindy used to ski at Mission Ridge as often as she could. She was eager to introduce Peter to the fun that could be had in this winter wonderland, although she was fairly certain Chad had taken his son sledding more than once.

They set a time to meet. Billy volunteered to drive, and then they would collect Peter together. Lindy connected with Ashley, who promised to have Peter ready before they arrived.

Thirty minutes later, Billy picked up Lindy. He greeted her with a warm kiss and hugged her mother. "My sister Dede's bringing her two little hellions and will meet us there," he told Lindy.

"What a great idea." She wished she'd thought to invite Dede herself. She'd seen Billy's sister at the Wine Press that one day, but not since then, and was eager to connect.

Her mother followed them to the front door and handed Lindy a thermos of hot coffee. "Have fun and stay warm," she said, sending them off.

When they collected Peter, the four-year-old was as excited as Lindy had ever seen him, running around Lindy like a cat chasing a mouse. While Billy moved Peter's car seat into his vehicle, Ashley gave Lindy an extra set of clothes and other essentials she thought Peter might need. Ashley figured Peter's energy would last until around noon, and then he'd be more than ready for his nap.

"Have a great time," Ashley said, standing in the doorway, waving to Peter as he dashed to the truck as fast as his short legs would let him.

"You ready for fun in the snow?" Lindy asked Peter, as she strapped him into the backseat.

Her nephew nodded vigorously. "I want to slide down the hill with the big kids."

"You got it, little man," Billy assured him.

"Billy," Peter innocently asked, as they headed across town, "are you going to be my uncle?"

Billy looked to Lindy and smiled. "I think your aunt should be the one to answer that," he said.

"Is he, Aunt Lindy?"

"Who told you that?" She had no doubt this came from Chad and Ashley.

"Daddy. He said Billy looked at you the same way he looks at Mommy."

"That's true," Billy said. "Your aunt Lindy is beautiful. It's hard for me not to look at her."

"I think you'd make a good uncle."

"Thank you."

Eager to change the subject, Lindy asked, "Where will we meet Dede?"

"I'll text her once we arrive at the park." Billy reached over and squeezed her knee, letting her know he recognized what she was doing.

It was a good thing they left early, as the parking surrounding the city park was at a premium.

Within minutes after their arrival, they found Dede and her two children. Davey was eight and Lily six. Lindy vaguely remembered Dede from her childhood.

"So glad we had a chance to connect," Dede said, once they were all together.

"I am, too."

When he was first introduced to the other children, Peter was shy and clung to Lindy. Before long, he was on the large sled with Billy and the other two children, squealing with delight as they soared down the slope. They repeated the ride several more times.

"My turn," Lindy cried, as she helped Billy haul the toboggan back up the hill. By cramming together, they were able to squeeze both adults onto the sled, along with the three children, with Billy taking up the rear position. When the sled started down the hill, she felt Billy's arms loosen from around her and then a cold blast of air as he tumbled off the back end, crashing into the dry snow.

Seeing Billy with his entire backside coated with snow had her bending over laughing. Lindy wasn't the only one who found humor in his predicament. The children and Dede couldn't contain their amusement, either. Their giggles floated in the air with the light flakes of falling snow.

"Very funny," Billy grumbled. He had nearly been buried in the white stuff. "You should be thanking me. If I hadn't let go, I would have taken all of you with me."

"We're eternally grateful, aren't we, kids?" Lindy did her best to look sincere. It had been heroic of him to take one for the team.

"Guess we know only one adult is going to fit with the kids," he said, as he, along with the children, continued to brush himself free of snow.

Lindy was happy to let Billy assume the duties. This gave her an opportunity to visit with Dede.

"Billy's been wonderful with Peter," she told Dede. Taking the thermos from the truck, she poured them each a coffee. They found a seat where they could view the hillside and watch as Billy trudged up and down with the kids. He not only hauled the toboggan, but he had both Lily and Peter on his back as he went. She was convinced this day would likely exhaust him. He was a good sport, lugging the kids up the slope.

"Billy's had lots of practice learning patience with my two," Dede said. She held the cup in both hands and looked down into the steaming liquid. "My brother is quite taken with you," she said, lowering her voice, as if she was hesitant to speak her mind.

"We've had a wonderful week," Lindy said, unsure where Dede wanted to take this conversation.

"So he said. I don't remember a time I've seen Billy this happy."

His sister's words warmed her. It had been a long time since she'd been this content herself.

"I know you're only in town on vacation," Dede continued, "and that you're going back to Seattle after the first of the year."

"Yes, that's the plan."

"And then?" She looked up and held Lindy's gaze.

"What do you mean?" she asked, swallowing tightly.

"What about Billy? Will you continue to see him?"

Lindy could only be honest. "I don't know. We're talking, and with his schedule and mine conflicting, we'll probably end up connecting via FaceTime or Zoom."

Dede nodded, as if she'd already heard as much from her brother. "You should know my husband and I took out a second mortgage on our home so Billy could move forward with the Wine Press."

Billy hadn't mentioned this. "That was generous of you."

Dede crossed her legs and her foot moved up and down

with what resembled nervous energy. "He needed some-thing after . . ." She paused.

"After what?" Lindy asked, certain Dede regretted speaking. She remembered Billy telling her he'd been dis-appointed by people he'd trusted. He'd never shared the circumstances and seemed reluctant to do so. "Did some-thing happen?"

Dede didn't bother to hide her surprise. "If Billy didn't tell you, then it isn't my place. You need to ask him your-self."

If he hadn't said anything, then Lindy didn't feel it was her place to pry. Naturally, she was curious and suspected it likely involved a woman. She'd shared her own broken heart, which didn't feel nearly as broken these days. If he'd held back his own heartache, she'd be disappointed in him.

"I've had my share of romances that ended with be-trayals and hurts," she told Dede, without going into any details.

"It isn't what you're thinking," Dede clarified. "I was wrong to have said anything." She avoided eye contact. "I need to be honest, Lindy. I have two major concerns when it comes to you and Billy. I hope you don't mind my speak-ing freely."

Lindy gestured toward her. "Please do."

"Thank you. First and foremost, please, whatever you

do, don't hurt my brother. He's had far too many disappointments in his life, starting with our father. Billy took it the hardest when our dad left. Like most children, he seemed to think it was his doing, that if he'd been a better kid, more well behaved, then Dad would have stayed."

Lindy nodded, understanding all too well that feeling of not being wanted. Everything changed for the better when Phillip Carmichael came into her mother's life. She had a father who genuinely loved and accepted her. Billy had never had that security and assurance.

"You said you had two concerns," Lindy said, urging Dede to speak frankly.

"Yes, well, I feel a bit uncomfortable mentioning this. I feel selfish even bringing it up."

"Please don't be. I'd rather you were honest," Lindy said, wanting to assure Dede she should speak her mind.

"I'm afraid Billy is so head-over-heels falling for you that he'll be distracted from the restaurant. My husband and I have invested everything we have in this venture and we don't want to lose our money."

"Of course you don't."

"I feel terrible even saying anything; I hope you'll forgive me. It's just that I know my brother. He rarely does anything half-measure. I don't know that I've ever seen him like this over a woman. He isn't going to want to let you go."

Lindy was at a loss for words.

"With you returning to Seattle and him stuck in Wenatchee, he's not going to be content with phone or FaceTime calls, he's going to want to be with you. I understand. When I first met my husband, he was serving in the army, and we were separated for long periods of time. I was miserable when David was stationed across the country and had to be satisfied with phone calls and emails." She looked up as if she expected Lindy to comment.

"I've been giving a lot of thought to the future," Lindy told her, without going into detail.

"I hope you understand my fears."

"Of course," Lindy said, wanting to reassure Dede she had no intention of hurting Billy. Nor was she keen on him risking his and his sister's investment in the restaurant. She was about to say more, when she noticed Dede's children racing toward them. Davey held on to his sister's hand as they stumbled through the snow.

Lindy was grateful for the interruption.

"We're hungry," Davey said breathlessly.

"And cold," Lily added.

"And Uncle Billy said he's tired." This, too, came from Davey.

Billy brought Peter with him, towing him on the sled, as he was too small to trek through the snow.

Dede immediately took charge. "Then let's get inside to warm our hands and tummies."

"Can we have cocoa?" Lily asked.

"I believe we can arrange that."

Rounding up the children, Lindy and Dede took over taking care of them. By then, Billy needed a break. They crossed the street, where there was a mom-and-pop diner. They went inside, removing their wet coats and heavy boots, and sat in a large circular booth. The children ordered hot chocolate that arrived with marshmallows melting on top.

Lindy could see that Peter was completely tuckered out. It was barely ten-thirty and she wasn't sure how much longer he'd last. Because of the other children, her nephew would never willingly admit he was exhausted.

Once everyone was warm and had their cocoa, the children were eager to get back on the sled. For another hour, they took turns riding the slopes, laughing and enjoying the day.

It wasn't long before everyone was pooped out. Before they left, Lindy hugged Dede.

"I appreciated our chat," she assured her, knowing Dede had been uncomfortable sharing her concerns.

Dede squeezed her back. "Thank you for listening."

As Ashley predicted, Peter instantly fell asleep once they were in the truck again and on their way back to his house. Lindy wanted to ask Billy about her conversation with Dede. Before she did, she needed to decide how best to approach the subject with him.

"It looks like you had a good time," Ashley commented as Billy carried Peter into the house and set him down on his bed. Peter didn't even stir.

Back in the truck, Billy turned to look at Lindy. "I saw you and my sister with your heads together," he said, his eyes full of curiosity. "What did she tell you?"

"As it happened, quite a bit." It was what Dede hadn't said that troubled Lindy.

"My guess is that she mentioned what happened in Yakima. It's painful to talk about it, to remind myself what a fool I was."

Lindy waited for him to continue. She wasn't going to pressure him, especially if he chose not to explain.

"Do you remember me mentioning how my friend Dan Berghoff was a mentor to me?"

She nodded, recalling how Billy looked relieved not to answer her question the night they'd had dinner in Leavenworth.

"I'd invested everything I had in another restaurant in Yakima with a partner, who was a former schoolmate of mine. I worked my tail off, while Kent was happy to give the responsibility to me. When I got sick and ended up having my appendix out, Kent emptied our bank account and split. I was never able to recoup. I lost everything, which is why I decided, with Dan's encouragement, to open the Wine Press."

"Oh, Billy, I'm so sorry."

"It was a hard lesson that I've put behind me."

She squeezed his hand, letting him know she understood that kind of betrayal, although it was different between her and Celeste. "I can only imagine how difficult it was to lose something you had worked so hard to make a success."

"I had no recourse. A legal battle would only have benefited the lawyers. I trusted someone untrustworthy and paid the price."

"How awful, Billy."

"I should have mentioned it earlier. Like you, I've had to let go of the resentment and bitterness. For a while, I decided to give up the restaurant business, unwilling to take another big financial risk. Dan was the one who talked me through my anger and frustration. Then Dede and David said they would be silent partners with me. Their faith in me to make the Wine Press a success meant the world. They believed strongly enough to give me the seed money necessary to start up. Thankfully, my reputation with the wineries in the state was enough for them to give me credit until I could repay them. And I have."

Lindy leaned her head against Billy's shoulder. He'd been through so much and come out both smarter and wiser. Looking back did no good. Not for Billy and not for her. They both needed to keep their eyes forward.

They both remained silent as Billy pulled into the driveway at her parents' house.

"Do you want to come inside?" she asked.

Billy shook his head. "I should probably check in with the staff. Can I see you tomorrow?"

"Of course."

"I'll call you."

That suited Lindy, who was ready for a long, hot shower and some downtime. Billy must run on adrenaline. He never seemed to stop.

Lindy spent a quiet evening with her parents and slept like a lamb through the night. She woke to a text message from Billy suggesting she stop by so they could have lunch together.

When her phone rang midmorning, she thought it was probably Billy, since she hadn't responded, wanting to check with her mother first.

Only it wasn't Billy.

"Lindy," her boss's excited voice shot over the line. "I couldn't wait to tell you. The Ferguson Group contacted us this morning and they want to go with your design."

Lindy's heart leaped into overdrive, roaring like an

Indy 500 engine. "They did?" She could barely speak, having lost her breath.

"They loved your proposal and are hot to get started. I know this is your vacation, I know we promised you two weeks. I feel bad even asking this of you, but is there any way you can cut it short so we can move ahead?"

CHAPTER SEVENTEEN

Lindy didn't know what to say. While she was thrilled and excited, she hated to leave sooner than planned.

"Like I said, we owe you this time off, but the company would be willing to amply compensate you for this inconvenience."

"It isn't the money," she said, and realized how badly she wanted to stay. Pressing her hand against her forehead, as if that would help her think, she had to remind herself this was what she'd always wanted, what she'd worked for all these weeks. This validation. This success.

"What would it take for you to return?"

"I'll be back tomorrow sometime," she said.

"Thank you, Lindy. You won't be sorry."

She sincerely doubted that was true. The call ended

abruptly, as if her boss was afraid Lindy would change her mind.

Like someone lost in a fog, Lindy wandered through the house until she found her mother.

Ellen stopped what she was doing and stared at Lindy. "Is everything all right, honey?"

"The Ferguson Group accepted my proposal. Now they want to get started right away, and my boss wants me to return to Seattle as soon as possible."

Her mother broke into an immediate smile. "Honey, congratulations. That's wonderful news . . . isn't it? I mean, other than you needing to cut your vacation short."

"I'm thrilled. I really am, although I hate that I have to leave so soon."

"I know. Dad and I will miss you."

"I'd better pack," Lindy said, and headed to her bedroom almost by rote.

"Do you need to leave right this minute?"

Some of the joy and pride in Lindy's accomplishment leaked from her voice, as if she was only now realizing the ramifications of this decision.

"I'm expected to be back in the office tomorrow."

"Oh. That is soon. I'm happy for you, only I hate to see you go." It went without her mentioning it that once Lindy was back in the office, it'd be long months of detailed work. Hours and hours at the office. Late nights, and often working one or both days of the weekends.

"What about Billy?" her mother asked, as Lindy reluctantly dragged her suitcase from beneath her bed.

"Billy," she repeated, with an instant sense of regret. "I'll have to let him know, and Peggy, too."

As soon as her suitcase was packed and loaded into the car, Lindy returned and hugged her mother good-bye. "Tell Dad and Chad, Ashley, and Peter good-bye for me. Tell them I'm sorry I had to leave in such a rush."

"They'll understand," her mother assured her.

"Lindy," her mother said, as she stood in the middle of the kitchen. Both hands reached for Lindy's shoulders and her eyes grew dark and serious. "Are you sure this is what you want?"

Her response was hesitant. "Yes. I think so," she said. "This is big for me. Really big. It is exactly what I've been waiting for all along."

Dropping her hands to her sides, her mother nodded, smiled, and hugged her once more before Lindy left the house. Her mother's question followed her. This was exactly what she wanted, she reminded herself.

On her way to the Wine Press, she phoned Peggy and told her the news.

Peggy congratulated her and then said, "I guess that

means my idea is off the table?" She made it a question, as if somehow Lindy might change her mind.

"For now it does, but that doesn't mean I won't reconsider later." Lindy hadn't given up on the idea, but the timing was all wrong for her to make that leap of faith now. She was in too deep with Media Blast.

"I'm going to miss you. I honestly hate to see you go."

"I know. I hate it, too. I'll keep in touch," Lindy promised, and hoped they would be able to maintain their friendship. Like anything else, friendship was an investment in time. Lindy couldn't help wondering how much spare time she'd have once she sank herself into this assignment.

"I'm holding you to that," Peggy said.

Telling Peggy she was heading back to Seattle was hard enough. She didn't know how she would manage leaving Billy.

Leaving her family.

Leaving Billy and Peggy.

Rolling into the parking lot at the Wine Press, she stood outside her vehicle while dread filled her. She should be over-the-moon excited, and in a way she was. She wavered between excitement and dread.

It was almost as if Billy had been waiting for her. He came out of the restaurant and met her outside.

Lindy couldn't see any need to delay the inevitable. "I'm heading back to Seattle."

"Today? Now?"

Lindy nodded, and felt the strongest urge to cry, which was ridiculous. She should be jumping up and down, cheering, jubilantly tossing her fists into the air.

Billy's face fell. "What? Why? I thought you had another week left of your vacation?"

"I do." She explained the phone call that had come in earlier that day. "It's the opportunity I've been waiting for my entire career," she said, as if she needed to remind herself. "I can't say no, Billy. Media Blast made an investment in me, and I can't let them down now. I'm sorry."

He nodded. "I understand." Then, without emotion, he added, "Go."

"This doesn't mean I won't be back," she hurried to tell him.

"Lindy, it's okay. Go. Like you said, this is what you've wanted your entire career. I understand. Yes, I'm disappointed, and yes, I hate that you're leaving, but I don't begrudge you your dreams."

Of all the things she expected him to say, this wasn't it. Deep down she'd thought . . . she'd hoped he'd plead with her to stay, to do whatever was necessary to have her come back so they could make a go of this relationship.

With her heart solidly lodged in her throat, Lindy turned to leave before Billy grabbed her and hugged her close for several long moments. He knew as well as she did that this was the end.

"It was fun while it lasted."

The finality of his words hit her hard. Was he really saying it was completely over? That what they shared was forever gone? Billy didn't really mean for them to make a clean break, did he? Lindy was convinced, as strong as their feelings were for each other, even in this short amount of time, that they'd find a way to remain in touch. Where there was a will there was a way, right?

The drive over the pass went without a problem, and she arrived in Seattle in record time. Once at the apartment complex, she unloaded her suitcase from the car and unlocked her door.

As she stepped into her home, it felt cold and empty. Standing in the middle of her living area, she looked around at the life she had built in Seattle. The contrast between the big city and Wenatchee, with those she loved most, couldn't have been more striking.

Peggy's disappointed voice echoed in her ear, and the look in Billy's eyes when she told him she was returning to Seattle haunted her as she went to bed that night. Before leaving Wenatchee, she'd grabbed the letter she'd written to Santa and read it again. She'd gotten everything she'd asked him to bring. A new best friend. A love interest. And that her proposal be the one accepted.

Her entire wish list was complete. She should be ecstatic, until she realized she would need to forsake the first two wishes in order to have the third.

First thing the next morning, Lindy arrived at Media Blast. After receiving a round of congratulations from her coworkers, she met with the Ferguson Group. Together with several of her own team, Lindy reviewed her proposal. The enthusiasm was high, and excitement filled the room.

After the lengthy session, Lindy knew she should be walking on air. This was what she wanted, what was important. Sitting at her desk, her thoughts weren't on the project, though, they were back in Wenatchee and all she'd left behind.

Being Peggy's roommate would be one crazy, fun-filled adventure after another. Lindy had never had a better friend.

And then there was Billy.

Her heart ached just thinking about him. She'd sent him a text late, before she'd gone to bed, which he didn't answer. She knew why. A long-distance relationship would be nearly impossible for them. He knew it. She did, too. But they could manage if they were both willing to sacrifice. Lindy was afraid Billy had chosen to sever all ties with her in order to protect his heart. She didn't blame him. He couldn't risk Dede and David's investment because of her, no matter how much he wanted things to work out between them.

Convinced once she was settled back in she would feel

more excited about the project, Lindy chose to ignore the voices in her head, telling her to follow her heart.

For the next several days, Lindy threw herself into the project, working long hours, putting in the sweat equity required. And this was only the beginning. There would be far more late nights in her future. At the end of the day, she checked her phone for text messages, hoping to hear from Billy. The silence ate at her heart. Peggy and Lindy exchanged several notes. She wanted to ask her friend about Billy, desperate to know if he missed her even half as much as she missed him. She didn't, though, and Peggy didn't volunteer any information.

On New Year's Eve, Lindy left the office later than normal and returned to her apartment with no plans in mind. No place to celebrate and, worse, no one to celebrate it with. If she was in Wenatchee, she'd be with Billy, and when midnight arrived, he'd take her in his arms, stare down at her, and smile before he kissed her into the new year. Instead, she'd spend the evening alone and miserable, wishing she could be with Billy and Peggy. Her friend had let her know she was headed to the Wine Press for a New Year's party with Jayne and Chloe, and several others.

As Lindy walked into her sterile apartment, things suddenly became clear. All this week, she'd pushed thoughts of Billy from her head and her heart. Only her heart refused to listen. Her heart knew exactly what she needed most. It should have been obvious. It wasn't until she faced that cold, dark apartment that she knew what she had to do.

Although it was crazy, even foolish, Lindy threw an overnight bag into her car and headed out. Because of the snow, Stevens Pass had chains required, but Snoqualmie Pass was open. Lindy didn't care how long it took; she was headed to Wenatchee.

The first call she made was to her parents. Her mother answered and Lindy blurted out, "Mom, I'm coming home."

"For how long?" her mother asked.

"I don't know, but, Mom, I think it just might be for good." As soon as she said the words, her heart sprang free. This was what she wanted most. Deep down she had the assurance she'd made the right decision. All at once she felt the crazy need to laugh. She inhaled oxygen into her lungs, and held it there as a sense of freedom filled her. It was as if she'd been walking around all this week in handcuffs, looking to make the most of what once had seemed important. Only Lindy knew now what really mattered. It wasn't proving herself to anyone at

Media Blast or accepting accolades from the Ferguson Group. It was being with those she loved, those closest to her heart.

Once she was on the road, she felt like everyone in the city had the same idea. The traffic was bumper to bumper. What helped her keep from growing frustrated and impatient was knowing she would bring in the new year with Billy. But at this rate, it didn't look like she'd arrive much before midnight.

Blizzard conditions had stopped traffic just this side of the pass with an avalanche warning. Lindy was stuck in it with everyone else, waiting for the all-clear sign before she could continue. An hour later, she was losing heart. She could be trapped here for heaven knew how long. While waiting, she called Peggy.

"Have you found a roommate yet?" Lindy asked as soon as her friend answered.

"No, why? Have you changed your mind?"

"Yup. It may take me a month to set everything into motion, if you're still willing to wait that long." Her friend was right, Lindy wouldn't have a problem subletting her apartment. As for Media Blast, the proposal was accepted, and the team would be able to follow through without her. Starting her own business would be a risk, but one she was willing to take. The benefits far outweighed the risk.

"Does Billy know?" Peggy asked.

"Not yet. I'm headed to the Wine Press as soon as I can get there. I'm on my way, only traffic is completely stopped."

"I'll be there."

"I know."

"You didn't tell Billy my suggestion, did you?" Peggy said.

"No."

"I thought as much."

"Why?"

"Billy's hardly been himself ever since you left. We both have been down. We decided to drown our misery together and were talking. I ended up telling him about my idea of you moving back, sharing an apartment with me, and starting up your own business. I don't think I've ever seen him more depressed. I wish I hadn't said anything."

"I'll explain when I see him." She'd do more than explain, she'd be sure he knew how badly she wanted to be with him, and that she was falling in love with him.

Peggy sighed into the phone. "You do that. I'm headed to the Wine Press for the party now."

"Don't let Billy know I'm coming."

"I promise I won't, but I'd sure like to see his face when you walk in the door."

"Say a prayer I make it. There's an avalanche warning in place, which means I could be stuck here for hours."

"I'll be looking for you."

It felt like a lifetime before traffic began to move again. Noticing the time, Lindy realized she should arrive close to eleven-thirty. New Year's had always been a fun time for Lindy. Like everything else, this year was different, and while it wasn't anything she had expected, she knew beyond a doubt it would be the best one of her life.

Her timing was perfect, and she pulled into Wenatchee with a half-hour to spare. Her parents knew not to wait up for her. Her mother said she'd keep the porch light on.

As she expected, the restaurant was busy and the bar crowded. She saw Peggy first, but not Billy.

Peggy rushed forward and hugged her. "I'm so glad you're here."

"Me, too." Even the thought of returning to Seattle the next day depressed her. Still, no matter the hassle of getting to Wenatchee, it was worth every minute as long as she saw Billy.

"Where's Billy?" she asked, looking around the crowd and not seeing him.

"I haven't seen him for a while," Peggy said, looking around.

"He must be in his office." Lindy headed in that direction.

When she walked into the kitchen no one raised an eyebrow. One of the chefs actually lifted his chin, indicating Billy was where she suspected.

A sense of anticipated happiness spread over her as she knocked at his door.

"Who is it?" he asked, sounding irritated.

CHAPTER EIGHTEEN

Instead of answering, Lindy opened the door. Billy looked up from his desk and wordlessly stared at her as if she were an apparition. He briefly closed his eyes before he slowly came to his feet and walked around the desk. It was almost as if he didn't know what to say.

"I wasn't expecting to see you."

"I know. It was a spur-of-the-moment decision." She noticed that he kept his distance. And she knew why, too. Billy didn't dare hope she was back for good this time.

"It's good to see you, Lindy," he said, placing his hand on the edge of his desk as if to steady himself. "I suppose you're heading back tomorrow?"

"Yeah, unfortunately. Media Blast is going to want at least two weeks' notice."

His gaze shot to hers. "You're giving your notice?"

"It'll take some time to find someone to sublet my apartment, so it might be longer than two weeks."

Billy's eyes met Lindy's, and it seemed to take an inordinate amount of time for her words to sink in.

"You're actually quitting your job?"

She nodded.

"I thought winning this proposal was a dream come true for you?"

"It thought it was, too."

"Then why are you walking away from everything you've worked this hard to achieve?" he asked.

"Don't you know? Can't you guess?"

Billy maintained his distance.

"Because I realize that everything that is important to me is right here."

Lindy couldn't understand why he hesitated. She expected to have been in his arms long before now.

"Do I dare hope I'm someone who's important to you, Lindy?"

It felt as if a giant vacuum cleaner had sucked all the oxygen out of the office.

"You should know, Billy Kincade, that you're the reason I felt the need to return to my roots, to my family, to my closest childhood friend. But far and away, I knew I needed to come back to the boy who claimed I'd written my name on his nine-year-old heart."

He came to her then, reached for her hand, and placed it over his heart. "Your name is still there, Lindy, and it's not going away."

"And neither am I," she promised.

He kissed her and it was every bit as good as she remembered. Every bit as wonderful as the first time during their sleigh ride.

Her face was flushed with warmth and love when they returned to the bar area where Peggy and the others sat waiting.

Just then the crowd started the countdown to the New Year.

Ten. Nine. Eight. Seven. Six. Five. Four. Three. Two. One.

Then Lindy was in Billy's arms. His lips were on hers as they brought in the next year together. It went without saying that this year and every year in the future, Lindy hoped to be spending with Billy Kincade.

Santa knew what he was doing when he told her she would have all her wishes fulfilled.

And she had far and above all she could have imagined or hoped for.

EPILOGUE

Lindy recognized the man in the red suit the minute she got into the line with the other mothers, holding their toddlers. She would always remember this particular Santa. He didn't seem to have aged at all since the last time she'd seen him, all those winters ago.

"Where's Daddy?" Adam, her three-year-old son asked.

"He'll be here soon." Billy had dropped her off at the Children's Closet, where Lindy had once had the role of Santa's helper, and now she was working with them as one of her many clients.

Sure enough, not more than five minutes later, Billy arrived, just in time for their son's turn to sit on Santa's lap.

Santa's eyes twinkled as he smiled first at Adam, and then Lindy. "And who do we have here?" the big man asked.

"This is Adam," Lindy answered, seeing that her son appeared unable to speak. The little boy, who resembled his father in so many ways, looked upon Santa with complete awe. His mouth hung open, and his gaze remained riveted on Santa's white beard.

"Well, hello, Adam," Santa said. "I know your mommy and daddy. Your mommy used to write me letters."

Adam remained speechless.

"What would you like for Christmas, young man?"

Without a pause, Adam said, "A brother."

Hearing him, Billy's eyes connected with Lindy's. "Guess we need to get to work," he mumbled, and gave her hand a gentle squeeze.

Santa glanced toward them and grinned. "I'll see what I can do, young fellow. Now, you be a good little boy for your mom and dad."

Adam nodded, and scooted off Santa's lap and hurried back to Lindy.

"Thanks, Santa," she said.

"You're welcome, Lindy." And then, with a twinkle in his eye, he winked.

The three left the store and headed across the street for hot cocoa before heading to Lindy's parents' for Christmas Eve.

"Did you hear Adam say he wanted a little brother?" Billy asked her after delivering the cocoa to the table.

"I did."

Adam looked from his mom to his dad. "Can I have a brother real soon?"

"I'd say in about eight months," Lindy told him.

Billy's eyes grew wide. "Did you say eight months?"

Lindy's face broke into a big smile. "I did."

Billy started to laugh, pausing only long enough to take hold of Lindy and kiss her.

"Daddy," Adam asked, "what do you want from Santa?"

"I already have everything I could have ever wished for," he told his son.

For that matter, so did Lindy.

Read on for a sneak-peek at
Debbie's new festive treat . . .

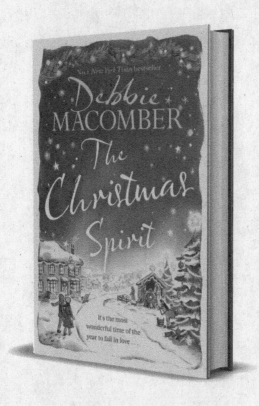

CHAPTER ONE

1977

"Hey, man, sorry I'm late," Hank said, as he slid into the red upholstered booth at Mom's Place across from his best friend. He was running on less than five hours' sleep, and his day was only getting started. "Did I keep you waiting long?"

"No, I was late myself." Pete had always been the responsible, prompt one. It surprised Hank to learn his pastor friend could be late for anything.

The waitress came with a coffeepot, and both men turned over the beige mugs to be filled. Pete smiled at her as she handed them menus and then swiftly left. Hank noticed how Pete's gaze lingered over the waitress as she returned to the counter and refilled another customer's cup.

"I'm telling you, these long hours are killing me," Hank said, as he wiped a hand down his face. His eyes burned, and he couldn't remember the last time he'd had a decent meal. As different as they were, they had continued a friendship after Pete had graduated from seminary and returned to Bridgeport. Pete looked every bit the pastor with his clean-cut looks, while Hank was often mistaken for a hippie, with his long hair and the casual way he dressed. Scruffy jeans and a T-shirt were his standard uniform, whereas he suspected his friend hadn't worn blue jeans since his college days.

Hank was the owner, manager, bartender, and chief bottle washer for the tavern The Last Call. Mom's Place, where they routinely met for lunch every month or so, was halfway between their two towns, Pete in Bridgeport and Hank in Kettle Springs. "I didn't get away from the tavern until after two this morning. Some days I swear I get less than three or four hours' sleep a night. This job's a killer."

Pete glanced up from the menu. "I thought you loved the tavern."

"I do. I always knew I'd be taking Dad's place one day. I looked forward to it. The regulars are great and keep me in the black, but I have no life. I haven't been on a date in six months."

"I'd think you'd meet women left and right," Pete said, before taking a sip of his coffee.

"I do. Lots of great women. I thought I'd be married and have a couple kids by the time I hit thirty."

"Why aren't you?" Pete asked.

Clearly, Hank's lifelong friend had no understanding of what managing a tavern entailed. "There's a big difference between meeting lots of women and having time to actually date. I work fourteen hours a day and sometimes longer."

Pete frowned. "Hire someone."

Hank snorted. Pete made it sound easy. "Do you have any idea how hard it is to find good help these days? I tried taking on a part-time bartender, and he drank all my profits. It's a slim enough profit margin as it is. At the rate he was drinking, I was about to go out of business. The thing is, if I need to be there to keep an eye on the staff, I might as well do without."

After a brief hesitation, Pete acknowledged Hank's dilemma: "Gotcha."

"Having my own business takes every spare minute I have. If I'm not at the bar serving drinks, then I'm in the office doing paperwork. Keeping up on the orders or dealing with the taxes. I swear it's one headache after another. Do you have any idea how much effort goes into the accounting aspect of being a business owner?"

"Well, yes . . ."

"Oh, come on." Hank gave a short laugh. "You're a pastor. The church doesn't pay taxes or struggle with money hassles."

Pete nearly spewed the coffee out of his mouth. "You have no idea! Pastoring a church is no walk in the park."

"Are you joking?" Hank was about to say more when they were interrupted by the waitress. He swallowed his argument and turned his attention back to deciding what he wanted for lunch.

Pad in hand, the young woman asked, "What can I get you gentlemen?"

Without looking up from the plastic-coated menu, Hank said, "I'll take the soup-and-sandwich special. On wheat, hold the tomato."

The waitress wrote it down, and he handed her the menu. Next, she looked to Pete.

"I'd like the chef salad," he said, "with Thousand Island dressing."

"I'll get that order in right away," she said, as she turned toward the kitchen.

"She's cute," Pete said, watching the young woman in the pink uniform with the white apron.

Hank frowned, his thoughts still on all he was missing in life. He caught his friend's interest in the young waitress, though, and played along. "Who's cute?"

"The waitress. It isn't any wonder you don't date. You

aren't paying attention. That woman is beautiful, and I noticed there wasn't a ring on her finger, either."

Pete was paying attention. Still, Hank let the comment pass. Pete should be the one married by now. He lived the good life and had none of the worries that hounded Hank from day to day. Hank envied him in that way.

Before Hank could encourage him to ask the waitress for a date, Pete said, "You should know my life isn't anything like you assume."

"Are you kidding me? Come on, Pete. You work your own hours . . ."

"That's not exactly true."

Hank dismissed his objection with a wave of his hand. "You get a steady paycheck every month."

"Yes, but . . ."

Hank wasn't listening. "Plus, the church provides you with your own house. No mortgage payments, no worries about making ends meet. And to top it off, you only need to make an appearance once a week. You're living the life, man."

Pete simply shook his head. It looked as if he was about to argue when the waitress returned with their lunch.

Again, Hank noticed the way his friend watched the young woman. It left him to wonder aloud, "Why is it you've never married?"

"Me?" Pete asked, as he mixed the salad and the dressing together.

"Yeah, you. Seeing how you made such a big deal about how easy it is for me to meet women, what about you?"

Pete looked like a deer in the headlights and then like a fish out of water, his mouth opening and closing several times.

"Not so easy to find the right one, is it?" Hank said, understanding all too well. "Church has gotta be full of upright, single, Christian women. You could have your pick of any one of them."

"I suppose," Pete reluctantly agreed. "The truth is, I don't know why I'm still single. I've had plenty of opportunity to date, but I've yet to find that special someone."

"I bet Gracie has something to say about that," Hank commented. Hank and Pete's sister had been at odds for years, always rubbing each other the wrong way. God save him from opinionated women. She was a spitfire, that's for sure. Frankly, Hank couldn't imagine how Pete worked with Gracie as his church secretary. She didn't have the personality for it, as far as he could figure.

"Gracie is Gracie," Pete said. "She's as righteous as ever. Stubborn as a mule and loyal as a dog."

"That sounds about right," Hank said with a snort. He smiled just thinking about her. She had her nose in the air and a holier-than-thou attitude. It was no surprise she hadn't married, either. Pete was nothing like his sister. His personality was perfect for his life's work. He was a caring, thoughtful man. Wise. Full of faith. Not that Hank lacked faith. He was square with God. But being a Christian didn't require him to show up for church every Sunday.

"You should know my job isn't all that wonderful, Hank. I have my own set of problems," Pete said.

"Sure you do," he said offhandedly. He didn't mean to sound condescending, but Pete had no concept of the demands on Hank's time and finances.

"It's Christmas in less than a week," Pete continued. "I'm running ragged getting everything organized. You, on the other hand . . ."

"What about me?"

"You party every night—"

"It's not a party," Hank interrupted. "I work hard to create a fun atmosphere but trust me it isn't always a party."

"So you say. You may work a lot of hours, which I don't discount, but you can sleep in each morning."

"Dream on," Hank said and rolled his eyes.

"And while you claim you don't have any time to date, which I have trouble believing, you have a chance every night to meet women."

"You have no idea what being a tavern owner means!"

"And you have no idea what the life of a pastor is like."

Hank laughed. "You couldn't do my job for a week."

Pete snickered. "You couldn't do *my* job for a week."

"Give me a break. You're living the easy life."

Pete set his fork down and leaned forward, his eyes intense. "You ready to find out?"

"What do you mean?"

"Fine, since you think I've got it so easy, let's trade places. I'll work at the bar and you fill in for me at the church."

Hank didn't hesitate. This was like taking candy from a baby. "You're on." He thrust his hand across the table. Pete extended his own hand and the two shook.

"Starting when?" Hank asked.

Pete's smile was wide. "No time like the present."

Oh, this was going to be good, Hank mused. Monday night. He was going to put his feet up and watch *Monday Night Football*, and for the first time in longer than he could remember. Better yet, he'd be able to pay attention to what was happening on the field.

Life didn't get any sweeter than this, and his friend was about to learn the biggest lesson of his life.

CHAPTER TWO

Grace Ann Armstrong glanced up from the typewriter when her brother returned from his lunch with Hank Colfax. Personally, she didn't know what it was about the tavern owner that appealed to Peter. Hank was the one who first shortened her brother's name to Pete, and soon all his friends followed, much to her consternation. As far as she could see, the two men had nothing in common, nothing that should bond their friendship, other than the fact that years ago they'd once played on the same football team and ran cross-country together.

Bottom line—Grace Ann didn't trust Hank. He was a tease and a flirt, and she wanted nothing to do with him when she was in high school, and even less so now. She did her best to hide her prejudice, although it was difficult not to share her opinion of her brother's best friend. The one time she couldn't help herself hadn't gone well. Grace Ann hadn't brought up Hank's name again.

"How was your lunch?" she asked, as Peter headed for his desk in the church office.

"Fabulous," he mumbled, sounding distracted. "What's my schedule like for the rest of the week?"

Grace Ann reached for the appointment book and reviewed Peter's commitments. "You're scheduled to pick up the mule from the Martin residence for the live Nativity scene. The Carney family is lending you their horse trailer."

"Why so early?"

"The Martins are leaving to visit their children. You promised to take Hortense for the week in exchange for her being part of the live Nativity on Christmas Eve."

Peter smiled, his eyes sparkling like he couldn't wait to pick up Hortense. "Wonderful."

That was an odd response. All those extra hours were sure to drain Peter's energy. "And of course, this is the week to deliver the charity food baskets, and then there's your regular visitation. Mrs. Millstone especially asked to see you this week. I set that up for tomorrow." That old battle-ax was a piece of work. How Peter maintained his patience with the woman was beyond Grace Ann. It was important that they pander to the former schoolteacher, as she had promised a hefty donation toward replacing the church roof, which was badly in need of it.

He arched his brows. "Right on." His smile grew even bigger before he slapped his knee and chuckled. "This should be good."

Grace Ann frowned and asked, "What's going on?"

"Nothing"—he hesitated—"of importance. I'll explain in a moment. Continue." He waved his hand, encouraging her to finish reviewing his calendar.

With each appointment she mentioned, her brother seemed to find nothing but delight. He couldn't seem to stop smiling and chuckling to himself.

"Anything else?"

"Well, yes, there's the possibility of a finance committee meeting. It was delayed last week because of the snowstorm. The last time I talked to Leonard, he insinuated it could wait until after Christmas."

For the first time since his return from lunch, Peter frowned. "Yes, make sure to delay that meeting until after Christmas."

"Okay, if Leonard phones, I'll let him know you want to put it off." Church finances were always a worry for her brother. She personally knew of twice in the last year when he'd taken less of a salary in order to meet the church budget. Grace Ann had offered to do without herself, but Peter wouldn't hear of it.

"That's it, then?"

"Yes." She glanced down at the appointment book to make sure she hadn't forgotten anything. "For now, anyway." As the week progresses, and seeing that Christmas fell on a Sunday, it would be double duty. Christmas Eve on Saturday night and then another church service on Sunday morning.

"Great," he said, when she'd finished. "It's going to be a busy week."

"Every week is busy." Peter was often exhausted by the end of the day. More than once, Grace Ann had encouraged him to find a helpmate. She did what she could to make his life easier. She was his sister, though, and what Peter really needed was a wife.

Grace Ann had lost count of the number of single women from the church she felt would be perfect for her brother. Godly women. He'd thoughtfully listened to her suggestions and had dated a couple of those she considered worthy candidates. Nothing clicked. She was discouraged, and it'd been a month since she'd last offered up another name. After all this time, she had no idea what Peter sought in a wife, because clearly they didn't share the same criteria.

One reason for her hesitation was Peter's interest in why she herself hadn't married. The majority of women at the age of twenty-eight in their community were married with children. A handful of the girls in her high school class had married the summer following graduation. After what had happened with Ken, she rarely dated. It was harder to meet single men in a small town. That, however, was only a small part of why she remained single. She wasn't about to marry just because that was what women her age were expected to do.

At the first of the year, she'd made a list of everything she wanted in a husband. She'd made the mistake of showing it to Peter, thinking it would help him in his own quest to find a wife. Her brother had read over her criteria, laughed softly, and then smiled before commenting, "It looks to me like you want to marry Jesus."

Grace Ann hadn't been amused.

"What are you up to this week?" he asked, cutting into her thoughts.

"Me?" she asked, surprised by the question. "This isn't an employee review, is it?" Peter would need to search far and wide to find anyone more dedicated to serving the church than she was.

"Not at all," he assured her, leaning against the side of her desk, as he looked over her side of the appointment book.

"Well, other than overseeing the office and answering phones, there's choir practice Wednesday evening." Holding her finger on the page, she glanced up. "It would be good for you to make a showing. The choir has given a lot of extra hours to ensure that the Christmas Eve service is everything it should be."

"I'll be more than happy to see to that." He nodded approvingly, as if adding an extra assignment to his schedule was exactly what he longed to hear. This was all so strange. Something was definitely up, but Peter was being tight-lipped.

"There's a Ladies Missionary Society meeting on Thursday." As president of the guild, Grace Ann had worked tirelessly to support those in the mission field. Both their parents were currently church planting in Costa Rica, dedicating themselves to the work of the Lord following retirement. Grace Ann was proud of her efforts, and the efforts of the other women of the church who'd given so much of themselves.

"I'll be cleaning the church before the service, of course." That was part of her regular duties. Peter often stepped in to lend a hand, which she appreciated.

"Put me down for that, will you?"

"Thank you, Peter." She found cleaning the toilets in the men's bathroom a challenge. The male youths were often off target when it came to their aim. Her brother had taken pity on her and had volunteered for the task, for which Grace Ann was most grateful.

"Make sure there's easy access to all the songbooks," he added.

"Of course." Naturally, Peter wanted everything perfect for the Christmas Eve service. Several in the community showed up at church only for Christmas and then Easter, as if that was enough religion to save their souls. Sort of like getting fire insurance before they met the Grim Reaper.

"I'll wipe down all the pews, too." Everything would be as spotless as she could make it. Grace Ann took her job seriously.

Peter showed his appreciation with an encouraging smile. Her brother was a gentle soul, caring and kind, unlike some friends of his she could mention. One in particular. She deeply admired her brother's Christian spirit, his willingness to dig in and give liberally of his time and himself. It wasn't beyond him to help those in need. He never complained or questioned when others called on him. He had a generosity of spirit she admired and often wished she could be more like him.

"I'll need you to type up a list of what's required of me for each day," Peter said, with what resembled a smug look.

This was the first time he'd ever asked her to do such a thing. They spoke each morning and reviewed the day's commitments as soon as they arrived at the church office, precisely at eight.

"Do you plan on being gone from the office?" she asked, thinking that had to be the reason for his request.

"As a matter of fact, I will be."

This was an unusual development, and one that came as a shock. "Where will you be?"

"Kettle Springs." His eyes sparkled with delight.

"Kettle Springs," Grace Ann repeated. "Why would you want to go to Kettle Springs?" Then it came to her. She should have guessed her brother's less-than-desirable friend had cooked up some dodgy scheme that would involve Peter.

"This has to do with Hank, doesn't it?"

"You could say that."

Exactly as she thought.

Whatever it was appeared to please Peter. Her brother was all smiles. Knowing him as well as she did, she noticed he seemed to be holding back the need to laugh, as if this was some sort of comedy in the making.

"Peter. Tell me. What's going on?" Whatever it was, Grace Ann was convinced she wasn't going to like it.

"I'll be tending Hank's bar."

"You're doing what?" She already knew this was going to be trouble.

"I'm going to work as a bartender for the rest of the week. Of course, I'll return in time for the service Christmas Eve and Christmas morning. Don't look so worried. This is going to work out beautifully."

"You can't do this, Peter. It's impossible." God help

them if anyone from the church learned about this. "Hank put you up to this, didn't he? Don't bother to deny it. This is exactly the kind of thing that . . . that Neanderthal would do."

"You worry too much," he said again, as if this was of little significance.

"Peter, you should seriously consider what you're doing." She needed a moment to clear the shock of this from her mind to help her brother understand the ramifications of this decision. "What if one of the church members hears of this?" She blurted out the first thing that crowded to the forefront of her objections. Peter simply had to listen to reason.

"What if they do?" he asked, completely unconcerned.

Her brother had lost his mind. She was astonished that he would be so blind to the risk he seemed all too willing to take. "You could lose your position."

"That's doubtful. Come on, Grace Ann, you're overreacting. It's only for a few days in another town twenty miles away. It's unlikely I'll run into someone from Bridgeport, and even if I do, so what?"

With her mind spinning, Grace Ann pressed her hand against her brow as if to help her sort through all the thoughts bouncing around inside her head. Her brother was delusional and required help. This was crazy, and from the look of him, she'd rarely seen him more excited.

"Do you think people who come into a tavern don't need God in their lives?"

"But . . ."

"It's the perfect opportunity for me to meet people who wouldn't ordinarily attend church."

"Ah . . ."

"Grace Ann, you're looking pale all of a sudden. Do you need some air?"

What she needed was for her brother to tell her this was all part of some silly joke. From the way he studied her, she could see that wasn't about to happen.

"I don't know what Hank said to convince you to commit professional suicide." Peter's friend was a constant source of irritation, and always had been from the time they were in grade school. He'd insisted on calling her Gracie, even though he knew she detested the name. This, though . . . this was above and beyond, she couldn't let Peter do it, for his own sake and the sake of his ministry.

"What about your duties here at the church?" Peter couldn't meet the needs of the church and at the same time work at The Last Call. It wasn't humanly possible.

"I've got that covered."

He'd found a substitute pastor? That seemed highly unlikely, especially at this late date. "Who's going to fill in for you?" she asked.

"Hank."

The breath left her lungs. Even before she could find the oxygen to breathe again, Grace Ann started shaking her head. This couldn't be happening. Hank serving as a pastor . . . She couldn't think of anyone less qualified.

"You're joking, right?" She sincerely prayed she'd misunderstood him and this was all part of a bad dream. If so, she wanted to wake up soon.

"No joke. I know Hank isn't your favorite person."

Her brother had no idea.

"How? Why?" At first, she'd assumed Hank had asked Peter to fill in as a favor. As an emergency.

"It'll be fine," her brother said soothingly. "We're trading places for a few days, that's all."

"That's all?" she repeated, too stunned to say anything more.

This was a disaster in the making and she wanted no part of it.

Debbie Macomber, the author of *Cottage by the Sea, Any Dream Will Do, If Not for You,* and the Rose Harbor Inn series, is a leading voice in women's fiction. Fifteen of her novels have reached No. 1 on the *New York Times* bestseller list, and five of her beloved Christmas novels have been made into hit movies. Macomber's Cedar Cove books have also been made into an original television series. There are more than 200 million copies of her books in print worldwide.

She lives with her husband in Port Orchard, Washington. Their children are grown and she is a proud grandmother.

debbiemacomber.com
Facebook.com/debbiemacomberworld
Twitter: @debbiemacomber
Instagram: @debbiemacomber
Pinterest.com/macomberbooks

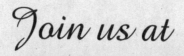